The Heart's Game

The Kelly Brothers, Book 4

by

Crista McHugh

The Heart's Game
Copyright 2014 by Crista McHugh
Edited by Gwen Hayes
Copyedited by Elizabeth MS Flynn
Cover Art by Sweet N' Spicy Designs

ISBN-13: 978-1-940559-94-0

Chapter One

"What happens at Comic-Con, stays at Comic-Con."

Jenny Nguyen repeated the mantra to herself before she adjusted the push-up bra that made her size A breasts look like overflowing C cups. One small pat smoothed her long green wig into place. The Sailor Pluto costume was a little on the immature side, but it was still adult enough to serve her purposes. She snatched the three condoms off the bathroom counter and tucked them under her bra strap before her courage faltered.

It was the last night of the San Diego Comic-Con, and she had only one mission. She was going to go outside her comfort zone. For once in her life, she was not going to be the good girl everyone expected her to be.

She was going to get laid.

Jenny grabbed the silver and garnet staff that completed her costume and ventured out of her hotel room. After enduring the cold, sterile process of artificial insemination ten days ago, she was determined to reclaim her femininity one way or another.

And hot, sweaty sex with a good-looking stranger seemed like just the thing to do it.

1

The hallway and elevator were empty as she made her way down to the lobby bar. Some of the crowds had thinned, many already on their way home after five days of utter geekdom. A majority of those who lingered were still in costume. She grinned. This was probably one of the few places where she could go out in full cosplay and not be considered a freak.

She scanned the crowd on the way to the bar. Like most cons, there was an overabundance of geeks and dorks she could probably have a great time talking to over a drink, but none of them got her blood pumping. Her limited sexual experience had been disappointing at best. The couple of men she'd dated back in college were about as adept in the bedroom as C3PO. No, tonight, she needed a real man. One who wouldn't blink when she suggested they hook up. One who would kiss her until she had no problem shedding her clothes and hopping into bed. One who would make her feel like a desirable woman.

But first, she needed to work up the nerve to voice that request.

She settled onto an empty bar stool and ordered a soda, wishing it was a shot of tequila instead. There was still a small chance she wasn't pregnant, but not small enough for her risk drinking. She owed her brother that.

As she sipped through the tiny bar straw, she watched the room from under the veil of her false eyelashes. There was a table of Trekkies nearby with one possible candidate. The group of Jedi knights were having too much fun with their fake light sabers to notice her, but a table full of teenage hobbits just outside the bar had no problem ogling her bare legs and overflowing cleavage. A flush stole onto her cheeks when they loudly started placing bets on what she'd be like in the sack. She was thirty, but she wasn't ready to venture into cougar territory.

Time to move to the other side of the bar.

She grabbed her staff and spun around, only to collide with a mass of muscle. Her soda splattered across her breasts, and her staff clattered to the floor. Her ankle twisted in her high-heeled boot, but a pair of steady hands caught her.

"Careful, Sailor Senshi," a deep voice with a hint of suppressed laughter said.

Jenny stilled and drew in a sharp breath. The warm scent of leather filled her nose, followed by notes of a spicy, masculine cologne. Her pulse jumped, and her skin tingled with awareness. She slowly lifted her gaze to look into the face of her rescuer.

Lines crinkled around a pair of bright blue eyes that complemented the amused smile on his face. He was dressed like Mal from *Firefly*, a true Browncoat down to the last detail, but she doubted Nathan Fillion looked this good in person. Her tongue tripped over itself as she stuttered, "Thank you."

His grin widened, but he made no move to let go of her. His gaze flickered from her chest back to her face. "Trust me when I say the pleasure was all mine."

Bingo! Perfect candidate for a one-night stand found.

Now she just had to gather up her courage to follow through with her plan without sounding like a desperate idiot.

He grabbed a few bar napkins with his free hand. "Sorry about spilling your drink."

Under normal circumstances, she would've taken the napkins and cleaned up the soda herself, but the image of him lowering his lips to her skin to remove the droplets off her breasts popped into her mind. A shiver coursed through her. Would he suck them up with teasing nips, or would he use long, languid licks?

She tore herself away from her fantasy long enough to realize he was still offering her the napkins and wearing that amused grin. As she took them and began dabbing up the soda, she began to worry if she was reading him wrong. Robots and code, she understood and could manipulate with the best of them. Men were an entirely different matter.

Well, at least he gets points for being a gentleman.

And his hand remained possessively planted at the base of her spine.

"If anyone should be apologizing, it's me," she managed to get out. "I was in such a hurry to move to a different spot—"

"I figured as much." His eyes flickered sideways to the table of hobbits. "I overheard what they were saying and was actually coming to rescue you."

Her nerves abated, and a smile tugged at her lips. "And do you think a Sailor Scout needs rescuing?"

"Depends on the Senshi. If memory serves me correctly, though, Tuxedo Mask was always swooping in to rescue Usagi."

"But as you can see, I'm not her." She ran her gloved hand along his brown coat. "And I think you're a little too casually dressed to be him."

"I left the tux and mask at home," he teased with a wink. "But why don't we move to the other side of the bar so I can at least buy you another drink?"

She bit her bottom lip long enough to quiet that little voice in the back of her mind that said good girls didn't hook up with hot guys they just met. She'd listened to that little voice for too long. Tonight, she was going to throw caution to the wind and finally know what it was like to embrace her sexuality. "That sounds like a fine idea."

"This way, then, Sailor Pluto." He took her staff and led her around the bar, his hand still on her back, pausing only a second to cast a threatening glare at the teens who'd been harassing her. That was all the time that was needed to silence them.

"Jameson on the rocks," he ordered as they settled into the new seats. "And what did you have?"

"Just a soda." When his brows furrowed together, she added, "I'm not much of a drinker."

He shrugged. "Fair enough. So, should I call you Trista or Setsuna?"

A giggle broke free from the tightness in her chest. "If I didn't know better, I'd say you were a covert fan of *Sailor Moon*."

He covered his mouth with an embarrassed cough and leaned in closer. "Shh, don't tell anyone."

"Your secret is safe with me." She crossed her heart and then lowered her eyes to the glass in her hand. "And actually, it's Hue, but you can call me Jenny."

The hard line of his shoulders eased, and he leaned on the bar, his upper body facing her. "Dan."

She peered up through her lashes. Her heart thudded in her chest like the engine to the *Millennium Falcon* when it was about to give out. This guy was seriously hot, and he seemed to be attracted to her. Normally, she was more of a wallflower than a centerfold.

All hail the effects of the push-up bra.

"Nice to meet you, Dan."

"So, where are the rest of the Sailor Senshi?"

Time to start playing the part of a seductress if she wanted to complete tonight's mission. She lowered her voice to a seductive purr. "They're in bed like good little girls."

He seemed to get her message loud and clear as his gaze flickered down her cleavage and back again. "And I take it you're not a good little girl?"

"Sailor Pluto is the oldest member of the Senshi." She stretched her legs out and lifted her chest. "A woman among girls."

Thankfully, he was looking at her as a woman.

Correction—as a woman he couldn't wait to get his hands on. His fingers blanched around his glass, and he licked his lips before taking a swig of the whiskey. "What are your plans for the evening?"

To ride you until I'm screaming your name when I come.

Jenny's cheeks flamed as the rogue thought ambushed her, and she focused her attention on the bubbles lining the inside of her glass. Being a temptress was harder than she'd expected it to be. Her whole life she'd been told to act modest and demure, to never engage a man for fear he'd assume too much. But tonight was her one chance to try something new and experience how it felt to be a bad girl.

"We'll see how the evening goes," she replied in a vague way that let him know she was open to suggestion without sounding desperate.

But she *was* getting desperate. Her body hummed like a horny teenager's. She wanted to touch him, to taste him, to run her hands all over him. Maybe it was the carefree con atmosphere. Maybe it was the pregnancy hormones kicking in, even though she had no idea if she actually was pregnant. Hell, maybe it was confidence bestowed upon her by the push-up bra. All she knew was that Dan had her ready to shed her panties faster than any man she'd ever met.

He stared at her for a moment and then nodded as though he'd read her thoughts and understood the turmoil raging inside her. "What was your favorite part of this year's Comic-Con?"

The nervous knot inside her stomach loosened, and the geek took over. She gushed about the costumes, the celebrity sightings, the films and panels. But unlike some other hot guys who'd seemed interested in her before, Dan's eyes didn't glaze over. Instead, he frequently interrupted her to add his own thoughts, sometimes even finishing her sentences. Her pulse quickened with each exchange, and she found herself inching closer to him as the conversation progressed. He didn't flinch when their knees touched, and when his hand grazed her thigh, it seemed as natural as breathing. Before she knew it, their heads were bent low, their lips inches from each other.

He reached up to tuck her hair behind her air, and her breath hitched. His touch was gentle, and yet set every inch of her on edge.

He grew serious, his attention fully focused on her face. "You're something else, Jenny."

"Meaning?"

"Just that. It's not often I meet an attractive woman who can quote *Next Gen* and give me the episode number it came from."

She gave him a nervous laugh and tried to look away, but his fingers ran along her jaw and guided her gaze back to him. "What can I say? I'm a geek."

"A very sexy geek." He closed the space between them by brushing his lips against hers.

The logical side of her brain tried to classify the kiss. It started out soft and respectful, more of an attempt to gauge how receptive she'd be. When she didn't pull away, the pressure became firmer. He was no longer seeking permission. He was seeking more.

And then all logic flew out the window as her baser instincts seized control. She parted her lips, allowing him to deepen the kiss. Warmth flooded her veins, and a haze of lust blurred her vision. This wasn't a virginal geek hoping to get lucky. This was a man who knew how to make a woman swoon with his tongue.

Jenny yielded even further to him, sliding off the bar stool and into his arms. The heat from his fingers penetrated her costume, practically branding her back through the thin cotton. She grew bolder, sliding her tongue into his mouth and taking her time exploring it while she slipped her hands under his coat and ran them over the hard planes of his chest.

A strangled growl rose from his throat, and he pulled

away, as breathless as she was. "We'd better take this somewhere else before we make a spectacle of ourselves."

"Agreed." But that didn't mean she had to move away. If anything, it made her move that much closer to him, pressing her body against him while he hastily paid the check.

"Where do you want to go?" he asked, his voice raw with need.

"I don't care, as long as we're not interrupted."

"My room, then." Dan took her hand and led her to the elevator.

Common sense made one final effort to stop her, warning her that he could be taking her up to his room to murder her or remove both her kidneys for the black market or a hundred other urban myths, but she easily suppressed it when she saw the bulge in his pants. This was good, old-fashioned lust at its finest. With any luck, in an hour, she'd be heading back to her room to sleep off one hell of a sex hangover.

Once the elevator doors closed, he pulled her back into his arms for one more searing kiss that made her toes curl. This was what she'd needed tonight. Even if the sex was subpar, she'd experienced enough heat and passion to remind her she was more than just a uterus.

As the kiss ended, she noticed something hard pressing into her thigh. "What is that?"

Dan gave her a sheepish smile and pulled out a red piece of plastic. "My lucky die. I never leave home without it."

Hot bod, awesome kisser, and a table-top player, too? Dan was everything she could've asked for in a man. She

9

stood on her toes to deliver a kiss that let him know in no uncertain terms how aroused she was, ending it as the elevator dinged. "Now that's sexy."

"You have no idea how turned on I am right now."

She grazed her fingers across the front of his pants. "I have a pretty good idea."

His room was only a few yards away, and she was back in his arms again. Behind closed doors, he didn't hold back. His hands were everywhere. Her ass, her breasts, her neck. She took a cue from him and shoved his coat off his shoulders before working at his belt next. They both had the same objective, and it involved getting naked as quickly as possible.

Dan found the snaps holding her costume together and had it over her head in a flash. He leaned in to sample her newly exposed flesh, but froze. He pulled out the condoms she'd tucked under her bra strap and held them up, one brow raised in a questioning manner.

Jenny crossed her arms across her bare stomach. "A good Sailor Scout is always prepared."

"My God, you're my dream woman."

The glow from his words turned into a raging inferno as he lifted her up into his arms for another kiss and carried her to the bed. A sharp tug on her wig left it in a jade green pool on the floor just before he laid her down on the mattress. Thirty seconds later, he'd stripped down to his underwear and joined her.

But as quickly as he'd removed the main parts of their costumes, he slowed down and took his time removing her gloves and boots. He seemed to want to taste and explore every inch of skin he uncovered. It was quite different than what she'd imagined would happen tonight. She'd pictured picking up some stranger for a quickie in a bathroom stall, not a leisurely love-making session. A mixture of impatience and appreciation rolled through her, for as much as she enjoyed his lavish attention, her body screamed for release.

It wasn't until he got to unhooking her bra that a brief moment of panic rushed through her. She tensed, and he paused to lift his head.

"Is something wrong, Jenny?"

Self-conscious shyness tempered her arousal. "It's just that I—I mean, the bra is a bit of an enhancer and I didn't want you to be disappointed and—"

He silenced her by covering her mouth with his, kissing her until her fears were forgotten. "Do you think I'd be any less turned on than I am now?"

She looked into his eyes and the desire simmering in them as he stared at her face. He wanted her, not her enhanced cleavage. A strange sensation bloomed inside her, one she'd never experienced outside the computer lab.

Confidence.

And it gave her the gumption to say, "Just hurry up and get inside me already."

"Gladly." He finished with her bra, and then followed by removing her panties before yanking off his boxers and unwrapping one of the condoms she'd brought. He settled his weight over her, the tip of his cock at the entrance of her sex. "Do you want it fast or slow?"

"I don't care. I just want you." She raised her hips and dug her fingers into his shoulders, fighting the urge to flip him onto his back and take control.

He chuckled and slowly slid into her.

Jenny drew in a sharp breath. He was long and thick, so much bigger than her previous lovers, and she was grateful he gave her enough time to accommodate him rather than slamming into her all at once.

"Let me know when you're ready for me to continue," he murmured, his expression tight with control.

The stretching burn faded, and she nodded her head.

A flicker of worry crossed his face. "First time?"

A full-bodied flush rose from her toes into her face. She shook her head. "No, I'm just not used to men as big as you."

He gave her a cheeky grin. "I'll still be gentle with you."

"Don't." She wrapped her legs around his waist and urged him to go deeper. "I want you to fuck me senseless."

"As you wish." He pulled back and slid into her again, increasing the tempo until he found a rhythm they both enjoyed.

Jenny followed his movements, her body rising to meet his in an instinctual dance known only to lovers. She ran her hands over the corded muscles of his back as they flexed and twisted with each thrust. She indulged in long, leisurely kisses that tasted faintly of whiskey and desire. She gasped every time his cock hit the sensitive spot inside her that sent an electric sizzle through her blood.

And she never felt more alive.

If this was her punishment for unleashing her inner bad girl, she'd gladly accept it.

Dan's strokes became faster, more erratic. It was a

startling contrast with the ever-increasing tension coiling inside her. Her muscles stiffened. Her breaths grew sharp and shallow. Her pulse pounded in her ears. And then everything collapsed in a rush that hit her harder than a dozen shots of a hundred and fifty proof liquor.

For years, she'd heard of the elusive female orgasm, but she'd never experienced one without the aid of a vibrator until now. *Explosive* was the only word she could use to describe it. Pleasure shot through her body with the force of jumping into warp five speed, followed by waves of smaller aftershocks. Her vision turned white. Her hearing dulled, but her other senses grew sharper. She could actually smell the seductive tang of arousal in the air and taste it when Dan gave her one final kiss before plunging into her and crying out her name. His cock throbbed inside her as he came, prolonging her own release until she was left in a dreamlike state of bliss.

She had no idea how much time passed, but when she came around, Dan's head was resting on her chest, his breaths still ragged. Her legs were tangled with his, and when she pressed her lips to his forehead, she tasted the salt of his sweat. A hum of satisfaction rose from her throat, and Dan lifted his head.

"Enjoy that?"

"Um-hm." She raked her fingers through his hair and bit her bottom lip. "Hopefully, I can stick around for seconds."

His eyes crinkled from his smile. "I'd like that."

"Good, because what happens at Comic-Con, stays at Comic-Con, and I intend to enjoy every second of it."

"Then I'll do my best to ensure that you do." His grin

13

widened, and he leaned forward to kiss her once again.

***

The warm body beside him shifted, then vanished. Dan cracked open one eye to spy a slender figure moving in the dim light of dawn. "Leaving already?"

"I have an early flight." Jenny bent down to retrieve her bra from where he'd tossed it last night.

"Where?" He blurted out the question before he could stop himself. He knew better than to get involved with a woman like her. A pretty face with a hot body and nothing between her ears was never a threat, but a fellow gamer would play him better than a level forty rogue. Cait had taught him that much.

And yet last night was the first time in years where he'd enjoyed a woman's company as much out of the sack as in it. None of the string of flings he'd had through med school and residency compared to Jenny.

She stilled, her face drawing as tight as her shoulders as she crossed her arms across her chest. "Listen, Dan, I had a great time last night, but let's just leave it at one night."

A fist of doubt punched his gut. "Shit, you're not married or something, are you?"

"No, no, no." She shook her head and seemed to shiver at the end. "I'm not involved with anyone. And to be honest, I'm not in a place where I could be."

"Why?"

She turned to the side and rubbed her upper arms. "It's complicated."

"Are you some secret spy like James Bond or Sydney Bristow?"

That got a laugh from her, and she sank onto the edge

of the mattress. "I only wish my life were that interesting."

"Then why the secrecy?" When she didn't answer, he pulled her back into his arms. He buried his face against the hollow of her neck, breathing in her exotic scent that reminded him of a Japanese tea garden. "Are you trying to tell me I suck in bed?"

"If you'd sucked, I wouldn't have gone back for seconds. Or thirds."

He pressed his lips to her neck, leaving a trail of kisses down it until he came to her suprasternal notch. Just talking about last night had him hard and aching for more. "Then how about fourths?"

"We went through all the condoms." But her body arched underneath him, undermining her words. She wanted him as much as he wanted her.

And her response to his touch almost made him forget about her warning. He needed to have her one more time before she disappeared completely. "Not all of them."

Her breath caught, but he couldn't tell if it was from his reply or that he'd just nipped her shoulder. "You were holding out on me?"

"I have an emergency condom in my wallet. Want me to fetch it?"

She licked her lips and nodded, desire darkening her already deep brown eyes.

He crawled out of bed and fumbled around in the dark until he found his pants. The condom in the back of his wallet had been there for months, but the wrapper still looked intact. He opened it up and slipped it on. "Thank God for backups."

She grabbed him and kissed him with a ferocity that

15

stunned him. The next thing he knew, he was flat on his back, and she was straddling his lap. "Then one more time."

"Gladly." He guided her hips so she was just about sitting on his dick and then lowered her onto him.

His breath entered with a hiss. The ultra-thin condom made it feel like he had nothing on at all, but a brief moment, he wished he could risk going without one. Then he could completely revel in her silky heat, savor the friction of every stroke, enjoy a woman in the most natural way possible.

And Jenny was a woman meant to be enjoyed. She pressed her palms against his chest as leverage while she rode him. Her head tilted back, giving him an uninhibited view of her breasts. They tempted him, called to him, and he sat up to take one in his mouth. A moan rose from her chest, and her slick walls tightened around him.

Dear God, he almost came right there. It was bad enough that he needed to remind himself she'd leave as soon as he did. These precious moments were a form of sweet torture, just enough to have a taste of paradise only to know it would be gone before he knew it.

"Dan." His name came out as a whimper accompanied by frantic rolls of her hips. She was so close to coming.

He reached between them and pressed his thumb against her clit, using the same rhythm she'd set as she ground against him. She gasped and clamped her hands around his cheeks, pulling him to her mouth for one more hungry kiss.

The burning at the base of his dick signaled the point of no return. He couldn't wait to come inside her, but not until she came first. He pushed hard, faster, deeper until she clenched around him and cried out with her release.

Fire rushed through his veins, followed a moment of panic. Everything felt too hot, too tight, too wet, as though the condom had vaporized. Jenny slumped against him, lost in her orgasm with his just a split second away. He cupped his hands around her ass and lifted her up as the first wave of cum shot out from the tip of the broken condom.

He'd gotten out in time, but just barely.

The panic faded, leaving behind the languid bliss that turned his muscles into Play-Doh. He fell back onto the pillows with her still in his arms. Her silky black hair fanned out across his jaw while her body trembled against him in a way that mirrored the quivering inside him. Yes, it had been risky to use the old condom with her, but in this moment, it was so worth it.

A few minutes passed before she lifted her head. "Now I really need to get going."

"I know." He cradled her face in his hands. "Are you sure you don't want to give me your number? We could maybe arrange for a little weekend getaway—no strings attached."

Her brows drew together, and her bottom lip jutted out ever so slightly. "No, I can't." She sat up and closed her eyes. "I'm sorry."

Her rejection stung harder than he thought it would, but he managed to nod and push his hurt into the pit of his stomach. Now came the awkward part of the conversation. "You wouldn't happen to be on the pill, would you?"

"What do you mean?"

He peeled off the ripped condom and held it up. "It seems we had a defective piece of equipment. I managed to pull out in time, but just as a precaution, I'd recommend picking up some Plan B as soon as possible. I got tested just last month, and I'm clean, but still..." And even though she didn't appear to be risky, he'd be getting tested again in a few weeks. One of the perks of being in the medical field—mandatory HIV and hepatitis testing.

She paled and nodded. "I'll keep that in mind. Do you mind if I use your bathroom before I go?"

His confidence took a blow. He'd fucked up, and his chances of making it right seemed almost as impossible as completing the Kessel run in twelve parsecs. "Help yourself."

Jenny gathered her things and dashed into the bathroom before he could stop her again.

Dan remained in bed, staring at the frame of light created by the closed door and wondering where things had gone wrong. He hadn't come to Comic-Con looking to score. Hell, he hadn't even considered taking Jenny back to his room when he'd first spotted her at the bar last night. And now she had him wanting to break all his rules and wishing he could have more than just one night of hot sex.

It was a dilemma that could only be resolved by one thing—a roll of his lucky die.

He found his pants and pulled out the twenty-sided piece of plastic. If he rolled high, he'd push one more time for her number or e-mail. If he rolled low, he'd let her go. He closed his eyes, asked his question, and tossed it onto the nightstand.

Ten.

Dan frowned. He wanted a clear indication one way or another, not a neutral response. He picked up the die and rolled it again.

Ten.

Fucking piece of plastic.

The bathroom door opened, and Jenny emerged, fully clothed. "Thanks again, Dan, for everything."

An uncomfortable ache formed in his chest, and he glanced at the lucky die one more time in vain hope it had changed to a twenty when he wasn't looking. "You, too, Jenny. And who knows—maybe we'll see each other at Comic-Con next year."

A weak smile formed on her lips. "Maybe so. But remember—what happens at Comic-Con, stays at Comic-Con."

A lump formed in his throat. His mind was screaming at him for letting her go like this, but he had to respect her wishes. He swallowed hard to shove the lump into his stomach. "Exactly."

She took a step toward him like she was about to change her mind, but then spun around and ran for the door like she was being pursued by a pack of direwolves.

The bang of it closing behind her echoed longer in his mind than it did in reality. He picked up the die and asked, "Did I do the right thing letting her go? High yes, and low no."

He let it go and checked the answer.

Twenty.

Shit.

He flopped back on the pillows and stared at the ceiling. His lucky die had never been wrong before. He just had to trust it and hope he hadn't made a huge mistake by not chasing after Jenny.

Chapter Two

"Wake up, sleepyhead," a deep, masculine voice cajoled.

Jenny opened her eyes and glared at the handsome black man leaning over her bed in the early morning light. "What are you doing here, Mike?"

He held up a rectangular box containing a pregnancy test and shook it like a child trying to guess the contents of his Christmas present. "It's been over two weeks. Time to see if we're having a baby."

Her pulse jumped, and she reached for a pillow to cover her face before he caught a glimpse of her panic. She already knew she was three days late, but she wasn't quite ready to confirm that she was pregnant. "I don't get out of bed before noon on Sundays."

"Well, tough, because your brother and I have an appointment with the interior decorator at ten for the nursery." Mike tugged on her arm until she sat up and then he shoved the test into her hand. "Now get in the bathroom and pee on the stick."

Jenny crawled out of bed and lifted her chin to make herself appear a few inches taller than five foot one, but

Mike still had a good foot of height and then some over her. Her brother's husband was built like an NBA player, but the intelligence gleaming in his eyes reminded her the man was as dangerous in the courtroom as he was on the basketball court. "Fine, but afterward, will you let me go back to sleep?"

"Of course."

She didn't bother tugging her T-shirt down to hide her Wonder Woman panties as she went to the bathroom. Mike had absolutely no interest in her as a woman unless it came to her uterus. After quickly reading the instructions, she took the test, set the timer on her phone, and waited for the results.

Sweat covered her palms, and her stomach jumped like she had a village of Ewoks dancing inside it. For only the second time since she'd agreed to be a surrogate for her brother and Mike, she questioned her sanity. The first time was when she forced herself to leave Dan's hotel room last weekend at Comic-Con.

The timer beeped, and she glanced down at the digital reading on the test.

Pregnant.

Her knees buckled, and she almost hurled on the spot. She sank to the floor and pulled her legs up to her chest, but that barely dulled the shaking that consumed her body.

Pregnant.

Shit.

A knock at the door kept her from falling into a full-blown panic attack. Her older brother, Jason, poked his head into the bathroom. "Jenny, are you okay?"

She blinked back the tears forming in her eyes. "Yeah,

just a little shocked."

Jason opened the door all the way and approached the test beside the sink. "It's positive?"

She hugged her knees tighter and nodded.

"It's positive," he shouted behind him.

A whoop of joy came from the bedroom, and Mike ran into the bathroom. "We're having a baby?"

"Yes, we're having a baby." Jason grinned like a new father and hugged his husband.

Jenny stayed where she was, wishing she shared their excitement. Instead, all she could think about was the life growing inside her and how she was responsible for it. What if she did something wrong and caused a birth defect or a miscarriage? What would she say at work when she could no longer keep her pregnancy a secret? And when the time came to give them their baby, would she be able to let it go?

Jason knelt beside her and threw his arms around her shoulders. "What's wrong, sis?"

"It's just not real to me yet."

"Aw, Jenny." He pulled her into a hug and soothed some of her worry. "Don't worry about a thing. We'll be right here for you."

Mike mirrored his husband on the other side, sandwiching her in a matching embrace. "What Jason said. You're giving us the one thing we can't have, and you have no idea how happy you've made us."

A choked sob broke free. "But what if I do something wrong?"

"Why on earth would you think that?" Jason stroked her hair and let her cry on his shoulder. "You're the smartest, most responsible woman I know. Why do you think we asked you to be our surrogate?"

She lifted her head and sniffed. "I don't know. Maybe because we share the same DNA."

"That's an added bonus." Her brother grinned and pinched her nose. "But seriously, there's no one we trust more to have our baby, and we are so grateful that you agreed to do this for us."

"So grateful that if you need anything these next nine months, all you have to do is ask," Mike added.

"Even pickles and ice cream at three in the morning on a Tuesday?"

They both laughed, and Mike nodded, giving her one more bear hug. "Yes, even pickles and ice cream at three in the morning."

An alarm interrupted their conversation. Jason pulled his phone out of his pocket. "Speaking of time, it's nine-thirty. We need to get going if we want to make our appointment in Belltown."

"I can't wait to start picking out things for the nursery." Mike placed a kiss on her cheek before standing. "I can't thank you enough for this, Jenny."

"That goes for me, too." Jason kissed her other cheek and squeezed her hand. "We'll see you at Mom and Dad's tonight and give them the happy news over dinner."

Oh, joy. She could only imagine what her mother would have to say about this. A wave of nausea rolled through her stomach. "See you then," she managed to say before her brother left the bathroom.

Mike and Jason left her condo in a flurry of excitement, but after the door closed behind them, she was left alone to digest the news. Her hand flew to her flat stomach. It seemed unreal there was a child inside there.

But for the next nine months, it would be hers.

***

Jenny parked her car in front of the white split-level home in Tacoma's Stadium District and groaned when she spotted the gold Lexus sitting in the driveway. Dì Tam, her mother's sister, was back from visiting family in Vietnam. That usually meant a chunk of the conversation would revolve around why Jenny wasn't married yet, followed by Tam suggesting some good Vietnamese men for her to marry.

What were they going to say when they learned she was pregnant?

She would've chuckled if it weren't for the fear she'd have both her mother and her aunt chewing her out for at least an hour.

The smell of *cha gio* frying greeted her when she opened the front door, along with the shrill conversation between her mother and aunt from the kitchen. Jenny listened long enough to realize they were gossiping about people they'd grown up with and decided it would be better if she didn't interrupt them. She tiptoed downstairs to the cool quiet of the basement. "Hi, Dad."

Her father stopped tinkering with the old motherboard long enough to lean into her hug. "Hi, Jenny. Does your mother know you're here?"

"Nope."

"Smart girl." He went back to the motherboard, his soldering iron in hand. "Think you can help me with this? Tam brought me this broken laptop and expects me to fix it."

She pulled up a stool and studied the intricate wires and circuits. She'd lost count of how many hours she'd spent at her father's side learning about computers. It was where she discovered her love for electrical engineering and what led her to follow in her father's footsteps. "What have you ruled out?"

"I think this diode overheated." He pointed the blackened blob of metal near the processor.

"And I'm sure that antiquated RAM isn't helping." She pulled it out and held it up to the light. "Does Tam realize it would be cheaper to buy a new laptop than try to bring this one into the twenty-first century?"

Her father chuckled. "But then she'd have to buy a new one when she can get me to fix this one for free." He picked up the broken diode with a pair of tweezers. "Can you grab me a half-amp diode from over there?"

She fished through the tiny bins of circuit board parts until she found the diode he wanted. "Did Jason tell you what he and Mike were doing today?"

"Nope. Just something about meeting with an interior decorator. I don't know why. They just got finished renovating that house on Mercer Island." He leaned back over the motherboard and started soldering the new diode into place.

She took a deep breath. "So they didn't tell you about our plan?"

"What plan?" he asked, never looking up from his work. "Are you moving in with them or something?"

"No, not that." She released her breath and wondered if she should spill the beans to her father first.

But before she had a chance, the basement door banged open. "Hue, are you down there?" her mother called from the top of the stairs.

She inwardly groaned. So much for avoiding detection. If there was ever a need for a cloaking device, it was now. Her mother was like a Klingon. No mercy for the weak. "Yes, Mom."

"Why didn't you come to the kitchen to say hello to me and your Dì Tam?"

Jenny shared a glance with her father as if the answer was obvious.

Her father chuckled and nodded toward the stairs. "Go on. I'll be up in a few minutes."

He didn't have to add that it would be to rescue her. Her parents were the living embodiment of the old saying about opposites attracting. Or, to take the Asian slant on it, yin and yang. Her father was calm and quiet, a man of few words with a Zen-like outlook on life. He firmly believed in serenely accepting what he'd been given and finding the positive in it.

Her mother, on the other hand, was like a swirling typhoon. Always moving. Always talking. Always wanting change. Instead of being content with what she had, she was always reaching for something newer, bigger, better. But it was her drive and seemingly endless energy that allowed their family to rise from their humble beginnings to the middle class life they enjoyed now. When she and her husband moved to the US from Vietnam forty years ago, they were newly married teenagers with only a basic understanding of English and barely enough money to pay for the evening's meal. Jenny's mom worked long hours, first as a seamstress and then in a nail salon, while her father got his engineering degree on a student visa. Now that her mom no longer needed to work, her time was spent meddling in her children's lives.

Jenny climbed the stairs and was met with a disapproving frown.

"What are you wearing?" her mother asked.

Jenny looked down at her T-shirt that read "Resistance is Futile (if <1 ohm)" and grinned. "Engineering joke."

"I told you to dress nicely."

"It's too hot to dress nicely." Especially when her parents lived in a house without air conditioning. After she'd managed to pull herself together this morning, she'd opted for comfort. A favorite tee, broken-in shorts, and flip-flops were the order of the day.

"You didn't even paint your nails." Her mother pointed at her feet and started jabbering in Vietnamese to Dì Tam about how children were lazy these days. "Go to your room. I have clothes for you."

Jenny knew better than to argue as her mother pushed her down the hall to the room where she'd spent her teen years. Little had changed since then. Math and science trophies filled the top shelf of the bookcase, with rows of thick fantasy and science fiction novels below. A *Mystery Science Theater 3000* poster with curling edges still hung on her wall between a *Star Wars* one and an autographed Jean-Luc Picard photo.

But lying draped over the bed was a bright pink *áo dài*.

She could already feel the tight confines of the dress squeezing her chest. "You're not expecting me to wear that, are you?"

"Dì Tam brought that back from Vietnam for you," her mother said with a heavy dose of guilt.

Jenny wrinkled her nose. "But it's pink."

"You look good in pink."

"Mom, how many times do I have to tell you that I don't like pink?"

"And that is why you don't have a husband." Her mother gave an exasperated sigh and shoved a bottle of pink nail polish into Jenny's hand. "At least paint your toes before dinner. We'll have a guest."

A mix of both English and Vietnamese curses formed on the tip of her tongue, but she bit them back like an obedient daughter. It was the thin line she always walked with her mother. She didn't want to completely rebel, but at the same time, she refused to be the demure daughter her mother wanted her to be. She'd paint her toes if that would appease her, but she drew the line at wearing the *áo dài* for a dinner guest. This was a family dinner, not a formal event.

When she reemerged from her bedroom ten minutes later, her aunt was gone. "Where did Dì Tam go?"

"To get some last minute things." Her mother forced a pair of bamboo chopsticks into her hand. "Here, stir the *bún.*"

Minding the boiling pot of vermicelli rice noodles was probably the only thing her mother trusted her to do in the kitchen. Too many hours in the basement equated to not enough time in the kitchen learning the intricacies of traditional Vietnamese cuisine. Jason was a far better cook than she was, and she suspected as soon as her brother arrived, he'd be recruited to assist their mom with the *bánh*

29

bột lọc lá.

Jenny tested the noodles for doneness and moved the pot over the sink to drain them. After rinsing them off with cold water, she turned to her mom. "Anything else?"

"Yes, you can go back to your room and change your clothes," she replied without pausing from wrapping the shrimp filled dumplings in banana leaves.

"Not happening."

Thankfully, the front door opened before an argument erupted between them. "Hi, Mom," Jason called from the entryway. He appeared a few seconds later in the kitchen to place a kiss on their mother's cheek. "It looks like a feast here. What's the occasion?"

He slid his gaze toward Jenny, silently asking if she'd shared their good news yet.

She shook her head as their mom answered, "Tam is back from Vietnam."

"And is that the reason you asked if I could leave Mike at home?" Disappointment mixed with a touch of anger laced his words. Although Jason was their mom's favorite, she'd never truly accepted his sexual preferences and only begrudgingly attended his wedding to Mike last year.

"Too many Vietnamese here," their mom replied without looking up from her work. "He'd feel like an outsider."

"Not if you spoke English around him. I'm trying to teach him, but there's only so much he understands." He moved from the kitchen island where their mother was preparing the *bánh* and jerked his head toward the backyard, signaling Jenny was free from kitchen duty. "Let me help you with these, *Má.*"

30

Jenny ran for the door before her mother found another reason to nag her and found Mike leaning against the deck, looking cool and collected in a pale yellow polo and pastel plaid shorts with a beer in his hand and a smug smile on his face. He offered her a soda pop from the ice chest beside him.

"You came anyway, huh?"

"One day your mother will succumb to my charms and good looks." He glanced down at her feet. "She made you do your toes again."

"As always." She opened the can of pop, but paused before she took a drink. "Do you think it's safe for me to drink this?"

"It's caffeine free and made with real sugar." He took a long drink from his beer. "Any reason why your mom asked me not to come tonight?"

"I have a sneaking suspicion it has something to do with Tam."

"She's back?"

Jenny nodded and took a sip of the pomegranate soda. "And I'm fully prepared for the matchmaking efforts."

"Just tell them you're gay," he teased with a wink. "That worked for Jason."

She laughed and leaned against Mike, enjoying the cool breeze that blew in from the water a few blocks away. "I have a feeling our news will have the same effect."

"Nervous?"

" 'Nervous' doesn't begin to describe it."

Her father joined them and fetched a beer from the chest. "Fixed it."

"Dì Tam will be so happy."

Her father nodded and flicked his gaze over her outfit. "So you didn't change your clothes?"

"Nope."

"Good girl. I like that T-shirt."

As an electrical engineer, he would. At least she had her father's approval.

Her father then started talking to Mike about his latest case. Both Jason and Mike were lawyers and worked at the same firm, although in different fields. Jason's expertise was in the field of environmental law, while Mike was a corporate litigator who handled the cases for some of the biggest businesses in Seattle. He divulged what he could, mainly that people were stupid, but steered the conversation toward the upcoming Seahawks season and how they'd defend their Super Bowl title.

Half an hour later, Jason joined them outside. "I've officially been banned from the kitchen." He took a beer from Mike and wrapped his arm around his husband's waist.

The list of reasons why was a mile long, from tampering with their mother's secret recipes to bringing Mike to dinner. "What for?" she asked.

"This time, for suggesting that you were quite capable of finding your own husband." He swirled the beer in his bottle. "I have the sneaking suspicion Tam left to fetch a potential groom for you."

They turned to their father, who merely shrugged in confirmation.

"Damn it!" Jenny slammed her can of soda down on the nearby patio table. "She knows better than to try that shit with me."

Jason took her hands and waited for her to calm down. "It'll be okay, Jenny. We've got this. Just sit between me and Dad, and we'll get through dinner without too much indigestion."

The front door opened again, this time with Tam proclaiming her arrival. Mom followed with the call for them to come in for dinner.

Sure enough, when they got to the table, there was a slender, well-dressed man in a dark suit standing next to Dì Tam. Her aunt gave her a strained smile and said in Vietnamese, "Hue, I'd like for you to meet Duong. He's from the same village your mother and I grew up in."

Jenny matched her aunt's smile, trying to not wince at the use of her Vietnamese name, and replied in English, "Nice to meet you, Duong."

Before her aunt could suggest she sit next to the potential bridegroom, Jason and Mike flanked her and pulled out the chair between them. "Let's have a seat and enjoy the delicious food Ma and Dì Tam made," her brother said.

Jenny sank into the chair and watched the frown deepen on their guest's face as he took in her appearance. No doubt he was promised a modest, quiet woman, not the sloppy girl in cutoffs and flip-flops. But it didn't matter. One way or another, he'd end up like the previous suitors her mom and aunt had tried to pair her up with.

Dinner was a tense affair. The conversation was mostly in Vietnamese, despite her and Jason's efforts to steer it back into English so Mike could follow along. Their guest's tight lipped disapproval only deepened with each course. He only spoke to Dì Tam or her parents and stiffened when he finally realized that Mike was Jason's husband. By the time they got to the *bánh bò* for dessert, he appeared to be forcing himself to endure their company.

That was when the matchmaking pitch began.

"Hue is an engineer," Tam started. "She makes very good money working for Microsoft and has her own home."

Which was code for "She's rich and has a place that could hold plenty of relatives." Jenny's cheeks burned, and she played with the sweet, flaky cake in front of her.

Duong nodded, some of the boredom vanishing from his eyes.

"Hue, Duong comes from a very old and respected family back home. He would make you a good husband."

Her stomach knotted, and she set her fork down. Time to let her aunt down gently. "I'm flattered he would consider me, but I'm not looking for a husband right now."

"But hue, you should get married before you get too old. You're already twenty-six."

"I'm thirty, Dì Tam."

Duong's eyes widened, and he turned to her aunt and said in a hushed hiss that he'd been told she was younger. The plot became clearer as the whispered conversation continued. He'd only agreed to meet her because she was a US citizen, and her confidence took another blow. She was nothing more than a green card to him, and even then, he was questioning whether or not she was worth it. She was too skinny, too slovenly, too outspoken. Embarrassment swirled inside her chest, bleeding out in her flushed cheeks until she could no longer bear it.

"I'm pregnant," she announced to everyone at the table.

Her mother and aunt wore matching wide-eyed, open-mouthed expressions of shock, but Duong managed to clamp his jaw shut.

"Are you just saying that to be difficult?" her mother asked.

Jenny shook her head and crossed her arms over her stomach. "I'm pregnant, and it's Mike's child."

That was the breaking point. Duong threw his napkin on the table and pushed his chair back in a huff, calling her a slew of insults that implied she had loose morals. Her mother and aunt rose with him, trying to convince him otherwise, but he was already headed for the door. The two women chased after him into the front yard, the slamming door finally silencing their pleas.

Jenny continued to stare at her half-eaten dessert and waited for her father to reprimand her.

Instead, he asked, "Was this the news you wanted to share?"

She nodded, unable to read his reaction from the tone of his voice.

Jason wrapped his arm around her shoulders. "A few months ago, Mike and I asked Jenny if she'd consider being a surrogate for us since she'd be able to give us the closest thing to our own child. She agreed, and we just found out this morning that she's pregnant."

Her father leaned back in his chair, his chin in his hand. "And you slept with Mike?"

Mike coughed and cleared his throat. "Actually, we did artificial insemination. I love Jason too much to cheat on him, especially with a woman."

"My confidence is really taking a nosedive here," she rebutted, her voice dry with sarcasm.

Mike placed a kiss on her temple. "I didn't mean it that way, Jenny. Next to my mama, you're the only woman I love."

Her father continued to mull over the information for another minute before nodding. "Then it is happy news. Congratulations."

Her father's calm acceptance contrasted with the banging of the front door and her mother's livid expression when she returned to the dining room. "I can't believe you would sabotage everything Tam and I worked so hard for. You had a man willing to marry you, and you had to announce that you're a slut who slept with your brother's husband. You have disgraced our family. Now you will never find a man who'll want to marry you."

She then ran toward her bedroom and slammed the door. Loud wails echoed through the house, and her father rose from the table with a heavy sigh. "I'll go talk to her. Once she realizes she'll finally be a grandmother, she'll be happy."

Jenny remained at the table, waiting for her parents to reappear, but her mother's angry shouts continued to come from the bedroom. After ten minutes passed, she decided it was time to leave. "I'm going home."

Jason and Mike nodded, holding hands as they stood, and followed her. "Just give Mom time," her brother said quietly. "Like Dad said, once it sinks in that she'll have a grandchild, she'll come around."

"I hope so."

But the sinking feeling in her gut warned her it would be a long time before her mother let her forget about this. She'd managed to make her brother and Mike happy, but she'd never felt more miserable in her life.

Chapter Three

Dan pulled his BMW into the empty driveway of a lakeside house and double checked the address. It matched the one his former college roommate had given him. Whatever Paul was doing, it was paying well, judging by the size and location of the Craftsman-style home. Dan grabbed his bag of dice and jogged to the front door, his step lighter than usual despite the busy week at his new practice. For the first time in years, he was going to enjoy a good afternoon of gaming.

His friend opened the door before Dan had a chance to knock and greeted him with the special combination handshake/high five/chest bump they'd created their freshman year at Northwestern. "Good to see you again."

"Same here." He made a quick perusal of the entryway of the house. "Impressive, man."

"Please." Paul waved him off. "I saw the house you grew up in. This is a shack compared to that."

"It's better than the place I'm renting." The surgery group he'd joined wanted him to start as soon as he was credentialed, leaving him very little time to find a place and settle in after finishing his residency. He'd started seeing patients the day after he returned from Comic-Con two weeks ago, and his apartment still was lined with boxes.

"For now, Dr. Kelly." Paul laughed and motioned for him to come upstairs. "The game room is this way."

He climbed two flights of stairs to an open loft space that had breathtaking views of the early afternoon sun glittering off Lake Sammamish. A large table dominated the center of the room, and at the end of it stood a full-scale replica of the Iron Throne from the *Game of Thrones* TV series.

Dan let out a low whistle and ran his hand over back, noting how it was made of fiberglass and not real metal. "Impressive."

"Yeah, you wouldn't believe how much my bank account whined when I ordered it." Paul settled into his throne. "But it suits me, right?"

Dan laughed. "Indeed. I suppose I should start calling you Joffrey now, huh?"

Paul wrinkled his nose. "Only if you want to lose your head."

The door opened downstairs, and three more people filed into the room, all in costume. Paul introduced them as friends and co-workers, but Dan immediately began sizing them up. A stocky guy and his wife were both wearing studded leather jerkins over green shirts, which he suspected made them more of a ranger or druid type. The other member of the game wore a long cloak and was as long and lanky as the wizard's staff he carried.

Dan rubbed his palms on his button-down shirt. "I didn't know I was supposed to dress up for this."

The jolly ranger, Derek, chuckled. "You're still new."

"Besides," his wife, Jessie, added, "we love getting dressed up for gaming. It's one of the things we look forward to every weekend."

And on the weekends he wasn't on call, he'd be looking forward to them too. Thankfully, he had several boxes of costumes to choose from.

Two more gamers arrived—a woman in a flowing medieval style gown and a guy in chainmail—but it wasn't until the sixth player arrived that his mouth went dry and his body froze with recognition.

It was the Sailor Scout from Comic-Con.

Only now, she was dressed head to toe in solid black with a pair of daggers on her belt and another peeking out from the top of her boot. Her long black hair hung in a thick braid over her shoulder, Lara Croft style.

The overwhelming urge to strip her out of her costume layer by layer filled him. He clenched his hands into fists to keep from stripping off those tight leather pants and plunging into her.

Her eyes widened when she saw him, and her greeting to the rest of the room halted mid-sentence. He caught the slightest shake of her head before Paul moved in to intercede. His old friend wrapped his arm around Jenny's waist, and a bout of nausea kicked him in the gut.

"Dan, this is one of my co-workers, Jenny." He gave her a jostling half-hug that shook away her shock. "Jenny, this is one of my good friends, Dan."

She gave him a tense smile and offered her hand. "So good to finally meet you, Dan. Paul's been anxious to add you to our game."

So that's how she wants to play it. Pretend like we're perfect strangers. And why not, especially since she and Paul were obviously a couple. He returned her smile and took her hand, squeezing it a bit harder than necessary. "Nice to meet you, too," he replied, fighting hard to keep his voice level. If there was one thing he couldn't stand, it was a cheating woman.

Paul glanced between them, his brows furrowed in worry. "Am I missing something here?"

The silent plea she sent him was enough for him to keep quiet. For now, anyway. "You know how I feel about rogue types." He gestured to her costume. "Am I wrong about the class of the character you'll be playing?"

Her grin widened to crinkle her almond shaped eyes, and the muscles in her forearm went lax. He could almost hear her silent thanks as she said, "Not at all."

"Jenny always plays rogues." Paul gave her one more hug before returning to his throne.

Dan stayed where he was, his gaze locked with Jenny's like they were two gunfighters in an old Western, and he was the one wearing the white hat. "Funny. I usually play paladins."

"Then this should prove interesting." Her expression remained wary as she moved to the empty chair between Jessie and the wizard boy.

Dan took the remaining chair across the table, studying her as they passed around character sheets and rolled the dice for ability scores. Paul talked about the characters and explained the world he'd created for this campaign, but Dan only half-listened. He was still trying to wrap his head around running into Jenny again.

Awkward didn't begin to describe it.

And judging by the way she refused to look at him, she was feeling the same way.

Time to set her on her heels. Normally, he chose to play a member of the warrior class that upheld the law and fought evil, but maybe it was time for a change. When it came time for him to declare his class, he stared directly at her and said, "Rogue."

Her lips parted, but her eyes glittered from the challenge. "There's usually only room for one rogue in our band."

"Then we can either work together or weed each other out."

Paul snickered from behind his DM board and scribbled something on his notepad. "I'm going to love this."

Dan crossed his arms and leaned back in his chair, hoping it concealed the rapid pounding of his heart. His D&D characters were lawful-good to a fault, and no doubt, Paul had created a campaign with some challenges fit for a paladin. Now he was going outside his comfort zone, but he still wasn't quite sure why. Part of him liked the idea of working closely with Jenny while another part of him was still recoiling from the possibility that she could be involved with his friend.

And if she was, would he be able to tell Paul about what happened at Comic-Con? After all, Paul had been the one who'd revealed Cait's infidelity.

42

Of course, Paul hadn't been the one who'd slept with Cait.

The tension started to ease as the game got underway. Everyone at the table was a skilled table-top player, each getting into character without venturing into the annoying territory most *n00bs* did. As the hours progressed, he could actually imagine himself going on a quest with them. Their skills complemented each other, and the feeling of camaraderie enveloped him as they accepted him as member of their group.

But every now and then, he caught himself watching Jenny. As soon as the game was over, he wanted answers.

Unfortunately, she dashed out of the room during the first break, and Paul intercepted him when he got up to follow her.

"Having fun, Dan?"

"Definitely." He glanced over Paul's shoulder one more time before giving up on going after her. "Do you mind if I ask you a question about Jenny?"

"She's not seeing anyone as far as I know, if that was what you were about to ask."

He released the breath he'd been holding. "So you two aren't...?"

Paul laughed and clapped him on the back. "Me and Jenny? No way! I know better than to date a co-worker, especially one of the most brilliant minds on my team." He dropped his voice and nodded to the woman in the gown. "Besides, I have my own thing going on with Gretchen."

"Good to know."

"Yeah, but keep it quiet, okay? I don't want the others

43

to accuse me of giving her special treatment."

"You mean the manticore you charged at her character wasn't your way of telling her you love her?" Dan teased. Learning Jenny was available gave him a whole different outlook on this game.

"Shut up." Paul's expression sobered as Jenny came back into the room, her face pale. "But if you're interested in her, don't treat her like your previous girlfriends."

Dan's spine stiffened. "Meaning?"

"I know your track record since Cait, and I don't want you doing the same to her. Jenny's a nice girl. Very shy. Maybe even a little innocent."

Dan resisted a contradictory snort. The woman he met at Comic-Con was anything but innocent. *Seductress* was a better word. A memory from that night flashed through his mind, and the blood rushed to his dick.

God help him, he still wanted her.

But judging by the looks she was giving him, she wanted him as far away as possible.

It tempered his desire. "I'll keep that in mind."

The game resumed, and he lost himself in the world of magic and mayhem Paul created. One thing he hadn't expected were the witty exchanges between him and Jenny. When she slipped into character, she became a whole other person. Fun. Flirty. Fearless. Far more like the woman he'd met two weeks ago than the shy girl Paul thought she was. If this was going to be their in-play dynamic, then he was definitely looking forward to each week's game.

He just wondered what it would be like if he asked her out after the game.

By the time the sun had set, his stomach was grumbling for something other than Cheetos and Mountain Dew. A glance around the table told him he wasn't the only one ready to call it a night. They all waited until Paul snapped his laptop shut and announced, "Till next week, adventurers."

Dan rose from the table and stretched, his attention so focused on Jenny that he didn't notice Paul coming up to him until his friend said his name.

"We usually head over to a local restaurant for dinner. Want to join us?"

"Sure." He watched Jenny out of the corner of his eye as she chatted with Gretchen and Jessie. "Where?"

Paul gave him the name of the place as he pushed him toward the door. "You can catch a ride with me."

He fought the urge to dig his heels in. If he was going to catch a ride with anyone, he wanted it to be her. "I don't want to be a nuisance."

"You won't be."

When they got downstairs, however, he noticed Jenny wasn't in their group. Dan turned around. "I think I left something upstairs. Go on without me."

"Fine, I'll see you there." He didn't miss the narrow-eyed look of warning Paul shot him before closing the door.

Dan found Jenny in the same place he'd left her beside the table. Her breath caught when she saw him, and her fingers blanched as they tightened around her dice bag. "What happens at Comic-Con, stays at Comic-Con," she said in a tense whisper.

"Maybe for most people, but this isn't that."

45

"No shit." She lowered her eyes and swiped her notes from the table. "We should get to the restaurant before the others worry about us."

He caught her by the wrist as she passed and pulled her against him. She was even more tempting than he remembered, and before he could stop himself, his lips were on hers.

She started at first, her back stiffening. A smothered cry of surprise rose from her throat. But a second later, the crash of dice rattled across the wooden floor, and her arms were around his neck. She teased the corners of his mouth with her tongue, begging him to deepen the kiss.

He opened his mouth to her and tasted the sweet remnants of the watermelon Jolly Ranchers she'd been eating all afternoon. The kiss was every bit as explosive as their first kiss two weeks ago. All traces of common sense fled his mind as the blood rushed to his dick. With their lips still devouring each other, he backed her up against the table, noting the small thrill when her legs wrapped around his waist. She wanted him just as much as he wanted her, so he was surprised when she planted her hands on his chest and pushed him away.

"We can't."

"Why not?" he asked before drawing the soft flesh at the bottom of her ear between his teeth.

"We could get caught." Despite her protests, she tilted her head back, exposing more of her neck for him to taste.

"They've all left."

"We shouldn't." Her arguments became as weak as the whimper in her voice.

He trailed his mouth along her neck toward her

shoulder. Time to convince her they should. "Tell me to stop, and I will."

A shiver rippled through her, and she gathered his shirt into her fists, pulling it out of his jeans. "I can't."

Objective unlocked! He cupped his hands around her warm leather-clad ass and pulled her even tighter against him. Her hips ground against him in a tantalizing rhythm. God, he couldn't wait to get inside her again.

There was just one small hitch. He lifted his head and asked, "Do you have a condom?"

She shook her head, and desperate disappointment filled her dark eyes. "Do you?"

"No." The word came out as a frustrated growl, and he let her go. The throbbing in his dick refused to ease, though. He refused to trust the condom hidden in the back of his wallet again. There had to be condoms somewhere in this house. "Wait right here. I'll be back."

She opened her mouth to say something, but he took off down the stairs to the middle floor before she had a chance to refuse him. If Paul had something going on with Gretchen, then he'd have condoms stashed somewhere. Thankfully, he found one in the nightstand and ran back upstairs, holding it up like it was the One Ring.

His jaw dropped when he saw Jenny. She'd stripped out of her costume and was sitting on the Iron Throne like a seductive queen with one slender leg draped over the armrest. She beckoned him closer and licked her lips nervously. "I hope you don't mind. It's a little fantasy of mine."

Damn! Could she be any more of my dream girl?

His mouth went dry. "Not at all."

"Then don't keep me waiting."

Dan shed his clothes in record time and fell to his knees in front of her like a worshipping subject. She was even more beautiful than he remembered. Her breasts seemed darker and fuller than before, rising and falling with each quick breath she took. Her skin was soft and silky under his hands as he explored her naked flesh. Her full lips practically begged him to kiss her again.

He'd never wanted a woman this badly.

But after being burned before, it was going to be on his terms.

He rolled the condom on and pulled closer until she was barely seated on the throne before grabbing her ankles and lifting them up to rest on his shoulders. If she wanted to be fucked on a throne, then he was going to enjoy it. He watched his cock slide into her, savoring every inch of her tightness.

Jenny gripped the arms of the throne and sucked in a tight breath through her teeth. "More."

He chuckled and took a moment to brace himself. She felt so good, he almost came right there. Combined with the visual of his dick firmly seated inside her, he was going to have a hard time lasting long enough to make her come if he didn't engage in some serious willpower.

He focused on establishing a tempo she enjoyed, varying the speed and depths of his thrusts until he was rewarded by the sweet sounds of her pleasure. Watching her enjoy him was a feast for the eyes. Jenny held nothing back. Her eyes were half closed, her lips parted and murmuring his name with every thrust. She arched her back so her breasts were inches from his lips, and he took the opportunity to nip one of her brown nipples, earning another moan of delight.

The pressure built up at the base of his cock too soon. He wanted to draw this out, to make her come again and again, but the warning bells in the back of his mind cautioned that if he didn't do something soon, he'd come before she did. He went deeper, harder, faster. Sweat beaded along his forehead and slickened his palms, but he was close.

So. Very. God. Damn. Close.

Her inner walls clamped around him, sending him over the edge as spasms of ecstasy started within her and flowed into him. Molten lava coursed through his veins as he came. He released her ankles as the strength fled from his muscles and he collapsed against her, burying his face between her breasts. The sated exhaustion that followed left him drained. He'd come hundreds of times before, but never quite like this.

Jenny combed her fingers through his damp hair. "We shouldn't have done this."

"Are you saying you didn't enjoy it?" He lifted his eyes high enough to gauge her response.

She gave him a sad smile. "I did. That's the problem."

"How is great sex a problem?"

"It can become addictive, and nothing's changed since Comic-Con. I can't get involved with anyone right now." She tried to push him off of her so she could stand, but he clasped her hands in his and held her prisoner.

Shit. He'd gotten so used to women chasing after him that he'd forgotten what it was like to have one push him away.

And he wanted Jenny.

Badly.

"Give me one good reason why we can't."

"For starters, it would throw off the whole game dynamic." She wrestled her hands free and continued to push him away.

"That's a bullshit reason, and you know it."

She managed to slip by him and began getting dressed. "And I hardly know you."

"That didn't stop you at Comic-Con."

"Comic-Con was an exception." She tugged her leather pants on, hiding her perfectly shaped ass from his view. "I'm not usually this type of girl, and I never expected to see you again."

"You're giving some of the lamest excuses I've ever heard." He rose from the floor, his legs still rubbery, and moved beside her. "What's the real reason you're pushing me away?"

Her whole body drew up like she was trying to hold back a stream of tears. "Please, Dan, don't keep asking me why. I just can't."

"Yeah, it's *complicated*. I know."

"There's no need to be sarcastic. If things were different, I would get involved with you, but…" Her voice broke, and she stared at the ceiling, blinking rapidly. "It's just that right now, the timing sucks."

No shit. He snatched his jeans off the floor and shook them out. He didn't dare ask when the timing wouldn't suck or if he should hold out any hope her life would become less complicated any time soon. He'd used the same lines enough to know she just wanted sex. Only now, he was on the receiving end of them, and it left a bitterness in his soul that called for a bottle of Jameson.

They finished dressing, neither one of them looking the other in the eye, and headed downstairs. Jenny got into her red Altima and took off without another word. Dan climbed into his BMW and drummed on the steering wheel, replaying what had happened upstairs. All he could think about was how awkward dinner would be with her there.

He pulled out his lucky die and asked, "Did I make a mistake hooking up with her? High, yes. Low, no."

Five.

Better than the ambivalent ten I got last time. He picked it up and said, "High, I should leave her alone and see how this plays out. Low, I should chase after her and demand answers."

Twenty.

Well, that's fucking clear.

He swapped the die for his phone and dialed Paul's number. "Hey, I'm feeling a bit worn out after this week and—"

"Don't tell me you're going to bail on us, too? Jenny just called and said she had a family emergency, so she won't be coming."

That's because she's already come. The image of her on the Iron Throne lost in her own ecstasy flashed through his mind, and he grew hard. He rubbed his eyes to erase the memories before he did something stupid like ask Paul for her phone number or address.

At least that solved one problem—he wouldn't have to pretend like nothing happened over dinner. "No, it's just that my mind blanked on me, and I forgot the name of the restaurant."

Once he got that info from Paul, Dan entered it into his GPS and followed the directions along the lake road.

It was probably a good thing she didn't want to get involved. Now he wouldn't feel tempted to break his own rule about never getting seriously involved with a woman, especially a fellow gamer. But the hollowness in his chest made him wonder if Jenny would be the one girl worth breaking the rules for.

Chapter Four

Shit! He's here.

Jenny popped a watermelon Jolly Rancher in her mouth to quell the rising surge of nausea that formed when she spotted Dan's car in Paul's driveway. Of course he would be there. They'd added him to their game. Worse, he was battling her for the team rogue.

She took a deep breath and blew it out through her nostrils. Combined with the hard candy, it usually seemed to quiet the morning sickness that had been hitting her with a vengeance. Thankfully, she'd only puked twice that week. The queasiness subsided, and she got out of the car.

Awkward or not, she wasn't going to let Dan keep her from enjoying a game she'd been a part of for the last five years. He was the newbie, not her.

After exchanging greetings with everyone, she settled into her chair across the table from him. Dan's eyes flickered to Paul's Iron Throne, and her cheeks immediately burned. She must have been suffering from pregnancy induced insanity last week. But as the heat in her cheek settled lower, the craving to have him again took over. She'd had a taste of great sex, and now she wanted more.

God, I'm like a friggin' junkie. I refuse to make the same mistake again.

Dan leaned back in his chair and gave her a smirk that told her he knew how much she wanted him.

Conceited prick.

But well earned. She turned away before she climbed across the table and propositioned him. *I refuse to make the same mistake again.*

The game got underway, and before long, she was presented with an opportunity to let her rogue skills shine.

"In the center of the room is a jeweled chest that is locked," Paul announced to the group.

"Jewels? As in treasure?" she asked. "Let me at that bad boy."

"I'd be careful if I were you," Dan replied.

"What kind of rogue are you?" she shot back, sinking into character. "It's free money, and I have just the set of lock picks to open it."

"And I still say you should proceed with caution." Dan leaned forward, his elbows on the table, locking his gaze with hers. "Don't you think it's a bit odd that someone would leave a treasure like this unguarded?"

Her head swam, and it had absolutely nothing to do with the game. She'd never realized how blue his eyes were. They rivaled the clear summer sky and sparkling lake outside, and she could easily get lost in them.

Of course, neither comparison helped ease her desire to get naked, damn it.

I refuse to make the same mistake again.

It took the equivalent of level twenty strength to turn

away from him and ask Derek, "Do you think you can cast a 'Detect Magic' on the trunk?"

Derek's ranger character did, and Paul revealed that the spell produced a moderate aura. Next to play was Sage, the group's wizard, who took it one step further and cast a spell that determined the spell was death magic.

Dan's grin turned smug, and he crossed his arms before leaning back in his chair. "Aren't you glad you didn't start picking the lock?"

Damn it, he was right.

As much as she wanted to be angry, her rebellious lips twitched in amusement. Dan was a better player than she cared to admit, which almost made up for the awkwardness of his presence. Maybe there was a chance they could pretend nothing ever happened. "Point made."

But I refuse to make the same mistake again.

***

Dan stepped out onto the deck and stopped short when Jenny's shoulders started to rise. Even though her back was to him, she must've sensed his arrival. He moved to the side, keeping a good five feet between them as he braced his hands on the railing. The afternoon sun shimmered off the lake, and a warm breeze ruffled his shirt. It reminded him of the summer days he spent at his family's cabin on Lake Geneva. "And I thought it rained here all the time," he murmured.

"That's what most people think of Seattle," she replied, staring straight ahead.

Her voice wobbled ever so slightly, but her shoulders loosened. Dan blew out a breath of relief. If he was going to get anywhere with her, he needed to make her relax.

And conversations about the weather seemed like a safe topic for now.

"Are summers always like this?"

"Most of the time, but you're almost always guaranteed to get rained on during the Fourth of July. But from the end of July to the beginning of October, it's really quite nice."

She still wasn't looking at him, but the corner of her mouth rose.

Dan reached into his pocket, squeezing his fingers around his lucky die. What he wouldn't give for a moment to ask it if he was on the right course. Instead, he had to rely on reading her voice and body language.

The breeze rippled her hair and sent a whiff of the soft scent of cherry blossoms he'd come to associate with her. He closed his eyes and breathed it in, his body coming alive as he remembered the last time he'd inhaled it. His gut knotted with desire and frustration. God, there was nothing more he wanted to do than pull her into his arms and have a repeat of last week.

But if he was going to trust his lucky die, he needed to be patient and wait for her to come around.

He just wished it wouldn't take so fucking long.

Time for another blasé conversation to knock the thought of sex from his mind. "So, you're not expecting any family emergencies this week, are you?"

Her cheeks reddened, and she rubbed her arms like she was cold, even though it was easily eighty degrees outside. "No, my brother said he would field any calls from my mother. She likes him better, anyway."

"You don't get along with her?"

Jenny shook her head, her gaze still focused on the lake. "I've tried to be the daughter she wants me to be. Quiet. Demure. Delicate. Graceful. Instead, I'm loud and awkward and much happier being single than settling for some husband she's picked out for me."

Finally, she was opening up to him. He took a small sidestep toward her, closing the gap between them by a foot. When she didn't flinch or move away, he said, "She doesn't like you because you're not married?"

She responded with a soft, self-deprecating laugh that made her head hang low before she lifted her eyes and turned her attention to him. "I wish it were that simple. It's a hundred other things, but let's just say I'm a disappointment when it comes to being an ideal Vietnamese daughter."

"Paul says you're one of the most brilliant engineers on his team. I wouldn't call that being a disappointment."

"But I'm thirty and not married, and I ruined her last attempt to pair me off with some green-card seeking douche to the scale of epic proportions. She's still not letting me live that down."

He took another step toward her, almost putting her within arm's reach. "When was that?"

"Two weeks ago. And last week, she was claiming that her heart was failing because of the huge burden of disgrace I'd placed upon it."

Now it was his turn to chuckle. "Sounds like she's a little dramatic."

"*Certifiable* would be more appropriate." Her smile faltered, and she lowered her eyes. "I wonder what she'd say if I told her about my behavior at Comic-Con."

57

The next step had him close enough that he could smell her scent without the breeze. He gripped the railing to keep from touching her, his knuckles turning white. "Remember, what happens at Comic-Con, stays at Comic-Con."

"True, but usually, hook-ups don't follow you home." She tucked her hair behind her ear and cast a sideways glance at his hands. "You know, I'm really not like that. I'm more like this. Shy. Awkward. Geeky."

"And what if I say I have a thing for shy, awkward geeks?" The words slipped out, followed by a punch in the gut. He'd sworn off that type of woman after Cait. And yet, he found something in Jenny that he'd been missing in all his flings.

A kindred spirit.

She gave him a sad smile tinged with regret. She didn't need to repeat that she couldn't get involved with him right now or that the timing sucked. He could read it in the fall of her hands and the shadows in her eyes.

He needed to take advantage of the progress he'd made before she slipped away again. "Jenny, I know you said you can't get involved with anyone right now, but I was wondering if maybe we can try to be friends."

A heavy pause answered him.

Each beat of his heart felt like it was ready to drum out of his chest. He hadn't been this worked up over talking to a girl since he was in high school, and that was only because most of the girls in his class were two years older than him.

At last, she nodded. "I suppose we could try that."

The heavy weight of anxiety lifted from his shoulders,

and he uncurled his fingers from around the railing. It wasn't exactly what he wanted, but it was a step in the right direction. Whatever her reason for pushing him away when it came to a relationship didn't affect his offer for friendship. And maybe, with a little time and patience, he could convince her they could be more than just friends. "Good."

"Hey, you two, enjoying the sunshine?" Paul said behind them, and they both jerked away from each other.

The tips of Jenny's ears grew red, and she let her hair fall forward like a curtain, obscuring her face.

He recovered faster than she did and pushed off the railing. "Yeah, you never told me how nice it was up here."

"Maybe I was trying to keep that secret all to myself." Paul gave him a playful shove. "You ready to come back in for some more magic and mayhem?"

"Sure," Jenny replied, pulling her hair back into a ponytail. Her timidity vanished as she slipped back into her rogue character. Her dark eyes glittered with mischief. Her posture straightened with confidence. And her inviting smile reminded him of the Sailor Scout who'd followed him up to his room last month for the one-night stand he couldn't forget.

This was the Jenny who drove him wild with lust, the one he wanted to know better.

Of course, the shy geek intrigued him also.

The question was, which one was the real Jenny?

His phone rang before he could decide. Adam's ringtone. That usually meant it was important. "I'll be up in a few minutes."

Paul and Jenny went back inside, and he answered the call. "What's up, Adam?"

"Have you seen the news?" his eldest brother asked.

"No, I've been gaming all day. Why?"

"Ethan found Ty dead this morning from what looks like an overdose."

The air whooshed out of his lungs, taking his lighthearted happiness with him. Ty and his younger brother, Ethan, had been best friends for as long as he could remember. They'd started Ravinia's Rejects back in high school after they'd gotten kicked out of a prestigious summer music program and had gone on to become one of the hottest rock bands in the country. They were as close as brothers, and he could only imagine what Ethan must be going through. "How's he holding up?"

"Not very well. Lots of blaming himself."

"It's not like he was supplying the drugs to Ty."

"No," Adam replied, "but we've all known for a while that Ty was in trouble. Ethan regrets not getting him treatment sooner."

"Just from my clinical experience, you can't force a person to go clean. They have to want it." Dan sank into one of the deck chairs and ran his fingers through his hair. "So what's he going to do?"

"Mom's flying out to LA to stay with him for a while and make sure he doesn't do anything drastic. Gideon's staying with him until then."

Of Dan's six brothers, Ethan was the most mentally unstable. He suspected his brother suffered from a mild form of bipolar disorder with all his highs and lows, but music had always been the one thing that kept him from

60

tipping too far either way. With the death of his band mate and closest friend, though, he might have lost his safety net. "It's hitting him that hard, huh?"

"Kind of hard to tell based on the conversation I had with him, but if you could call him later tonight and check in on him, maybe give us your professional opinion—"

"I'm a surgeon, not a shrink. I cut people open for a living. I don't mess with that mental stuff."

"But at least you were exposed to it in med school, unlike the rest of us."

Dan groaned and stared up at the clear blue sky. The sunny day was in complete opposition with the dark news his brother had just given him. "Fine, I'll check in on him because he's my brother, but remember, I have my limitations. If Mom thinks he needs help, she'd be better off finding someone there to take him on."

"Thanks, Dan."

"Sure." He hung up the phone before Adam asked another medically related question. That was the problem with being the doctor in the family—he was always getting hit up for his medical opinion. Often times, it included a huge helping of too much information, like the time when Frank sent him a picture of his dick and asked if it looked like he had herpes.

After spending a few minutes trying to figure out the best way to approach the conversation with Ethan, he dialed his younger brother's number.

"Hello," Ethan answered in a flat voice.

"Hey." His throat closed up after that. Somehow, starting the conversation with "I heard you found your best friend dead with the needle still in his arm" was not the best tactic.

Dan cleared his throat and said, "I heard the news. How are you doing?"

"How the fuck do you think I'm doing?"

"I can only imagine." He paused. "Do you want to come up here for a bit? It's actually sunny here in Seattle."

"No." The single word sounded like it came from a snarling dog with its haunches raised, and Dan decided to back away.

"Okay…" And he thought his conversation with Jenny had been difficult. "Well, if you need a change of scenery, my door's always open. I remember that you always liked the music scene here."

"I just want to be left alone. Between you and Gid and Adam and Mom and the fucking mob of reporters outside, I can't even get a moment to myself."

"We're just all worried about you. Well, maybe not the reporters. More like the family—"

"I got it. Don't worry. I'm not going to drive my car off a cliff or shoot up some heroin."

Dan's chest ached from the grief in his brother's voice. Ethan was trying to sound tough, but he was suffering deep inside, and there was nothing Dan could do for him from this part of the West Coast other than say, "I'm here if you need me."

"Thanks. If I need my appendix out, I know who to call."

"I didn't mean it that way."

Ethan hung up before he could get another word in.

Friggin' asshole.

His anger evaporated, though, when he rationalized

that this was Ethan's way of handling bad news. Throughout his medical career, Dan had seen the rainbow of responses, everything from depression to anger to acceptance. His brother had been living in the tough as nails rocker world for so long, every conversation seemed to be wrapped in barbed wire lately.

Dude needs to get laid.

Dan pulled out his lucky die and said, "High, I should call him later tonight. Low, I should leave Mom to deal with him."

Six.

"I can handle that." He stowed the red die in his pocket and went back to the game, but every so often, he reached for his phone to make sure there wasn't a text message from his family giving him an update on Ethan.

Chapter Five

Jenny added a new line of code to the firmware she was working on and crossed the lab to see if it fixed the bug. She tapped her fingers on a drawing of piano keys, playing the melody of "Für Elise." In the plastic case in front of her, a robotic hand copied her movement on the synthesizer with the same precision, filling lab with beautiful music.

Someone applauded behind her.

Jenny whirled around to find Paul leaning in the doorway. "Tell me what you really think," she teased.

"Fine." He came over and played the *Star Wars* theme using the visual input robotic device. "Now *that's* fine music."

She laughed. "Maybe for Jedis in training like you."

"Who said anything about me being a padawan?" He waved his hand in front of her face like a Jedi master. "You will accept me as your Sith Lord and join the Dark Side."

"Only when you pull me out of Star Fleet Academy."

"Damn you, Trekkies," he mocked, Shatner-style. "Speaking of eternal geek debates, what's going on between you and Dan?"

Her shoulder blades drew back as through he'd poked the spine between them. Did Dan tell him about Comic-Con? "What makes you think there's something going on between us?"

"Oh, please! Dinner Saturday night was like watching a documentary on flirting. We were all taking bets on whether or not you two would leave together or separately."

"Well, as you saw, we left separately." She hit save and started cleaning up her work area, hoping Paul would take a hint and drop the subject. The last month had been an exercise in self-control. She knew better than to get involved with Dan, especially since she was already in the middle of week ten of her pregnancy and wouldn't be able to keep it a secret much longer. Once he learned of her surrogacy, he'd take off running just like Duong.

But that still didn't stop her from wanting him.

Only now, she wanted him for reasons outside the bedroom. He was fun to be around. He got her jokes and didn't seem to look down on her for being a geek like him. And he'd never once tried to press for anything more than friendship on her since that first game four weeks ago.

"Yeah, I was kind of disappointed by that. Your debate with Dan was epic."

"I think I proved my point that the technological advancements of the *Star Trek* universe made it a far superior series over the likes of Jar-Jar and Jedis." She made a show of straightening the few pieces of paper on her desk. "Besides, to quote Han Solo, 'Hokey religions and ancient weapons are no match for a good blaster at your side, kid.' "

Paul grinned and shook his head as though to say he had nothing left to add. Instead, he sat down in her chair and rocked from side to side. "But seriously, why are you turning Dan down?"

The papers slipped from her fingers, and panic crept into her throat. "He told you that?"

"Yeah. I nudged him to ask you out, and he said he already had, and you said no."

"What else did he tell you?"

"That your excuse was bad timing." He stilled and nodded to the robotic hand. "I know it's not due to work because you're already ahead of schedule on this project."

"Paul, please, don't get involved—"

"I'm not trying to stick my nose where it doesn't belong, but I will vouch for Dan. I've known him for over ten years. He's a great guy, one of my best friends, and I'm glad to actually see him serious about someone after his years of playing the field."

"What makes you think he's serious about me?"

"He hasn't lost interest in you." Paul pretended to pick a piece of lint off of his immaculate button-down shirt. "He normally stays away from girl gamers after what Cait did to him in college, but from what I've seen, he seems to want to make an exception to the rule when it comes to you."

A sinking feeling settled into the pit of her stomach, and possibly for the hundredth time since Comic-Con, she cursed her luck. Of course she would meet the perfect guy when she was knocked up with her brother-in-law's kid. But that still didn't stop her curiosity. "What happened in college?"

"He and Cait dated all through college. He was even getting ready to propose to her. Then I happened to catch her with someone else and told him." He shrugged like he'd caught her at the grocery store instead of in another man's arms. "Since then, he's never dated a girl longer than a month, and even then, they were more fling material, if you know what I mean."

Sort of what I was like at Comic-Con.

Of course, she'd been after the same thing. Just a fling. Nothing more.

"Paul, I really appreciate you trying to play matchmaker, but I'm going to tell you the same thing I told Dan. This is just not a good time for me to be getting involved with anyone."

"Fine. I'll back off. But if you change your mind, here's Dan's number." He pulled a slip of paper from his shirt pocket and placed it on her desk. "In the meantime, get out of here. It's Friday night. You should be having fun, not sitting around in a lab. See you tomorrow afternoon for the game."

After Paul left, Jenny stared at the paper with Dan's number like it was a viper poised to strike. And for all she knew, it could be just as dangerous. The physical longing for him roared to life just like it had four weeks ago. She'd been so good about keeping it under wraps, so good at confining it and pretending it didn't exist. But now that she had the means to discreetly satisfy her hunger, it overwhelmed her.

She picked up the paper and read the number. It would be all too easy to call him up and invite him over to her place. If what Paul was telling her was true, then maybe he'd be open to a purely physical relationship. And when she could no longer hide her pregnancy, she could end it. She doubted it would be hard to do. After all, her encounter with Duong proved to her that no man wanted to be involved with a woman who was pregnant with someone else's child.

But for now, she could satisfy her physical craving for him.

Once she got her nerve up to call him.

She grabbed her phone, her thumb hovering over the digital keypad.

And then she chickened out.

I have no clue how to initiate this. It's not like I'm an expert on booty calls.

And yet, the few times she had told him what she wanted, he was more than happy to oblige.

Texting will be safe. Less pressure. Less awkwardness if he turns me down.

She switched over to her messaging screen and typed in his number, followed by:

Dan, this is Jenny. Do you want to come over to my place tonight?

Her heart fluttered in sync with the nauseating butterflies in her stomach. She read the message one more time to make sure it didn't reek of desperation. Then she hit send.

Less than a minute later, her phone buzzed.

Her hands shook as she opened the message.

When?

She covered her mouth to smother a yelp of joy. He

wasn't going to turn her down. Her fingers flew over the screen.

How about in an hour?

His reply was almost instantaneous.

What's your address?

Her mind reeled. Holy crap! She'd just propositioned a guy, and he accepted. She'd never done anything like this. Well, except for Comic-Con.

She sat down before her knees gave out from under her. Condoms. She needed to pick up condoms on her way home from work. But after that...

Her nipples hardened, and the place between her legs began to tingle with anticipation. She was going to get laid, and by a man who knew how to make her come.

She glanced down at the message and typed in her address. Then she grabbed her backpack and ran out the door. She had just enough time to grab a box of condoms and clean up her place before he arrived. And then, with any luck, she wouldn't be leaving her bed for the rest of the night.

***

Dan parked his car in one of the guest parking spots at Jenny's condominium complex and took a deep breath. He'd been half hard since he'd gotten her text an hour ago, and he needed to get a better grip on himself before he crossed the line. An invitation to come by her place could mean a number of things from "Hey, let's get naked" to "Hey, let's watch *Star Trek* all night." Not that there was a problem with either one. Jenny was cool enough that he'd have fun with the latter, but his evening would be infinitely better if it was the former.

69

Still, after weeks of her pushing him away, it was good to actually have her wanting to see him outside the game.

Just don't assume too much.

He grabbed the takeout he'd gotten on the way over. Dinner would help soften the blow if she was only looking to hang out and maybe make this feel like more of a real date. He checked his appearance in the mirror, noting the dark circles under his eyes from being on call the night before. Thank God he'd managed to get a nap this afternoon, or he might risk falling asleep as soon as he got to her place. He found her door and knocked.

Jenny opened it a few seconds later and grabbed him by the shirt, hauling him in and slamming the door before locking her lips with his.

His dick sprang to life. *Oh, yeah!*

The bag of pho slipped from his fingers, and he threaded one hand through her hair while cupping a breast with the other. The passion of her kiss, the hungry moans, and the way her body melted against his left no doubt in his mind why she'd invited him over. But despite the burning desire rushing through his veins and heading straight to his cock, a little voice in the back of his mind was shouting "Danger!" like that annoying robot from *Lost in Space*.

It took a Herculean effort to pry his lips from hers and ask, "I thought you wanted to be just friends."

"I changed my mind." She tugged his shirt over his head and ran the flat of her tongue over his nipple.

The ache in his cock doubled, but somehow, he managed to keep his head on straight. "About not getting involved with me?"

She froze, then took a step back. Her lips were red and full, her cheeks flushed. Her unbound breasts rose and fell with each quick breath, and her pebbled nipples underneath her thin tank top practically begged him to take them into his mouth. By God, she was tempting. The perfect portrait of a woman consumed by lust. But her eyes remained guarded, and she shook her head. "No, that hasn't changed. But I was hoping you'd consider a friends with benefits arrangement."

"So just sex?"

She nodded. "Nothing more."

"And what if I want more?"

"That's all I can give you right now."

No strings attached sex. That has been his MO for years. One fling after another. Always losing interest and going after the next thrill. But now the tables were being turned on him. And while any red-blooded guy in the world would be thrilled with what Jenny was offering him, there was a small part of him that wanted more.

Shit. I'm turning into a woman.

He ran his fingers through his hair, at an unusual loss for words. And he could only imagine what her response would be if he pulled out his lucky die and asked it if he should take her up on her offer. This time, he was forced to trust his gut.

Jenny took another step back. "While you're making up your mind, I'll be getting naked in the bedroom."

She whipped off her tank top, giving him an eyeful of her luscious breasts, before turning around and disappearing into the next room.

The throbbing in his cock intensified to the point

where all he could think was, *I'd be a fool to turn this down.*

He unzipped his jeans and followed her. And who knew? Maybe after a few nights like this, he'd be able to convince her that they could be more than just friends with benefits.

Chapter Six

The sound of the front door opening pulled Jenny from her sex-induced coma. Her heart jumped into her throat, and panic drove away all the lovely sensations that lingered from the sinfully hot naked man sleeping next to her.

"Hue," her mom called out, "where are you?"

Fuckin' hell!

Jenny bolted from the bed, rousing Dan in the process, and grabbed her bathrobe.

"What's wrong?" he asked, his eyes still groggy.

Shit, shit, shit, shit, shit! Leave it to her mother to ruin a perfectly beautiful morning.

"Hue, are you still sleeping?" her mother shouted.

"Who's that?" Dan asked.

"My mom. Just stay here, and I'll deal with her."

She ran out the door before her mother barged in and found Dan in her bed. It was bad enough Vietnamese people didn't bother calling ahead of time before coming over. But if her mother caught Dan, she'd never hear the end of it.

She slipped out of the room, closing the door behind

73

her, and tried smoothing out her snarled hair. "Mom, what are you doing here?"

Then she noticed Jason standing behind her mother and the amused glint in his eye.

God, I must look like a nymphomaniac. Not that it was far from the truth. Dan made ample use of the condoms she'd bought last night.

"I was going to Chinatown with your brother and wanted to invite you to come along."

Which meant she'd gone out of her way to come by her place. It was the first time her mother had said something halfway nice to her since she'd ruined the matchmaking efforts. "Gee, Mom, you could've just called."

"Why do I need to call? You're not doing anything this morning." Her mom stopped and pointed to Dan's shirt on the floor. "You are too messy. No wonder you're not married."

This morning couldn't get any more humiliating. She swiped it up before her mom realized it wasn't hers. "It must have fallen out of the laundry basket."

"And there's perfectly good pho by the door. I put in the kitchen for you to eat later."

Her stomach rolled. If the pho had been sitting out all night, she wasn't going to take a chance on getting food poisoning by eating it. She was already puking enough from the morning sickness. "Thanks, Mom."

"Let me pick out something for you to wear."

Jenny's pulse went into overdrive as her mom reached for the doorknob, and she plastered herself to the bedroom door. "Really, that's not necessary. I'm a big girl, and I can dress myself."

"But I want you to look nice in case we meet a good Vietnamese boy for you in Chinatown."

I wonder what would happen if I told her I spent the entire night fucking a white boy.

"Mom, if that's the reason you want me to go to Chinatown with you—"

"Why are you not letting me into your room?" Her mother tried to grab the knob again, but Jenny continued to block her. "How messy is it?"

"*Very* messy." Rumpled sheets, tossed clothes, naked man...

"Then I will clean it for you while you get ready."

"No, Mom, please, I—"

Her words died in her mouth as the door gave way behind her, and she stumbled back into a hard, warm bare chest.

If ever there was a need for a wormhole to swallow her up, it was now. Or maybe a Tardis...

Her mother's eyes bugged out, and her jaw dropped. Jason coughed to cover his snicker.

"There's my shirt." Dan took it from her and bent to place a kiss on her cheek. "Thanks for finding it."

"Who is that?" her mother whispered in Vietnamese.

Time for the most embarrassing introductions in my life. "Mom, Jason, this is Dan. Dan, this is my mother and brother."

Unlike her family, Dan seemed to remember his manners. "Nice to meet you."

When they still didn't respond, he tilted her chin up and placed a quick peck on the tip of her nose. "I'll see you later this afternoon."

"Okay." *If my mother doesn't kill me first.*

Her mother and brother parted to let him pass, still trapped in stunned silence.

But as soon the door closed behind him, the spell was broken, and her mother started screeching in Vietnamese, "What was that man doing in your room?"

A sting of irritation formed at the base of her neck. A few weeks ago, she would've respectfully lowered her eyes and pleaded for forgiveness from her mother, but since she was already on a crash course for being disowned, she might as well say what was on her mind. "He was sleeping before you barged in and woke us up."

"He was sleeping with you." Her mother pointed a single finger at her, but it was full of censure. "First, you sleep with your brother's husband, then you sleep with a white boy?"

"Just to clarify, she never slept with Mike," Jason interjected, but their mother drowned him out with a string of Vietnamese curses.

After hearing her mother call her a slut and a disgrace, Jenny stopped listening. She crossed her arms and sank onto the sofa while her mother circled the room, vocalizing her anger and distress to the walls.

Jason plopped down next to her. "He has a cute butt."

"You would notice that."

"I'm an ass man," he said with an unapologetic grin. "So, tell me a little more about him."

Jenny couldn't help but notice her mother's rants began to quiet, her ear turned toward them so she could pick up any details.

"He's Paul's old college roommate."

"And?"

"And he just moved up here and joined our game." She didn't dare tell them about Comic-Con. Her mother had never understood her fascination with cosplay, and she didn't want to give her the wrong impression that cons were little more than orgies.

"What else?"

"He's a doctor."

That shut her mother up. She came to the sofa, the sly smile on her lips complementing the scheming light in her eyes. "What kind of doctor?"

"A surgeon."

Her mother nodded. "A surgeon is good."

"Yeah, too bad he's a white guy, and I'm nothing more than a slut, eh, Mom?"

The smile slipped from her mother's face, and the ranting revived at full force.

Jason gave her a playful nudge. "Nice comeback."

"Maybe I'm getting a bit cranky in my old age."

"Don't forget hormonal from the baby."

"How can I forget that?" Her stomach was already churning. She grabbed a watermelon candy from the bowl on the coffee table and popped it in her mouth. "Calm her down before the neighbors complain. I'm going to take a quick shower."

"So you're still coming with us to Chinatown?" her brother asked.

"Sure, as long as my slutty presence won't disgrace the family."

"Mom will get over it." He dropped his voice and added, "Besides, I want more details on this guy. I think he's the first guy you've ever had over to stay the night."

"So? I'm allowed to enjoy a night of good sex, aren't I?"

Jason's grin widened. "Just good?"

She laughed. "Try mind blowing."

"I thought as much. And he's cool with you being pregnant?"

The happy glow faded. "Um, I haven't told him about that yet."

"Well, you're going to have to do it soon."

"I know, I know. Just give me some time to sound him out first." *And enjoy a few more nights in the sack with him before he runs away screaming.* "I'll be out in a few."

"I'll take care of Mom." Her brother crossed the room to their mother and began speaking in soothing tones.

Jenny turned on the hot water and let the shower beat down on her knotted shoulders. The water streamed down her overly sensitive breasts and along her still-flat stomach to the pleasant ache that lingered between her thighs. She had enjoyed last night. Almost too much. It was going to make it that much harder to sit across from him today and pretend they were just friends.

She just couldn't risk losing her heart to him, though. It was just sex. Nothing more. After all, when he learned the truth, he'd want nothing more to do with her.

Chapter Seven

Jenny opened her eyes and rolled over to the side of the bed Dan slept on just like she had every morning for the last three and a half weeks. The scent of his cologne lingered on his pillow. She hugged it and took in a deep breath through her nose, a flush washing over her body when she remembered the rough quickie they'd had this morning. She'd woken up just as he was getting out of the shower and pulled him back into bed for a round of fast, pounding, toe-curling sex before he left for the hospital.

As she came to the end of her first trimester, her morning sickness was giving way to a severe case of morning horniness. Thankfully, Dan had been more than happy to oblige her demands. He'd slept over almost every night since she'd invited him over, and it was nights when he was on call that she missed him the most.

She paused and loosened her hold on the pillow. Damn, she was getting used to him being in her bed. She enjoyed their conversations in the wee hours of the morning about the meaning of the Borg or how Peter Jackson had managed to ruin *The Hobbit*. She was getting spoiled by the great sex on demand. And she was running out of time. It wouldn't take Dan long to realize that she hadn't gotten her period since he'd started sleeping with her, and then she'd have to reveal the truth that would end the seemingly perfect arrangement.

Of course, if she didn't tell him soon, he'd find out on his own and probably be angry with her for deceiving him.

It was a classic *Kobayashi Maru* situation—one she had no chance of winning. And unlike James T. Kirk, she had no idea how to cheat.

The buzz of her alarm interrupted her thoughts, reminding her that her personal life would have to be placed on hold until she got home from work. She crawled out of bed, saw the dried blood along her inner thighs, and sank to her knees.

Oh, shit! Oh, shit! Oh, shit!

Blood like that could only mean bad news when it came to the baby.

She fumbled for the phone and dialed her OB's office, only to get a recorded message telling her they were closed. She hung up and doubled over, paralyzed with fear, her heart pounding in her chest and making it nearly impossible for her to draw in a deep breath. Dan was a doctor. She could ask him what to do, but in doing so, she'd have to reveal she was pregnant. But none of that mattered to her anymore. The most important thing was the baby.

Her breath caught. *What if this was all my fault?*

A sob tore through her. All this time, she'd been cursing the fact she was pregnant because it was keeping her from having something more with Dan. And now, when she was faced with the prospect of actually losing the baby, all she could do was wonder if her reckless abandonment in the bedroom had caused this. What if the quickie she'd had this morning triggered a miscarriage?

The images of the disappointment on Jason's and Mike's faces flashed before her. They would be crushed if she lost the baby they wanted more than anything in the world. How could she tell them it was because she was being selfish?

She picked up the phone and dialed her OB's office again, this time staying on the line long enough to hear the option to page the doctor on call. She left a message with the call service and dashed to the bathroom to scrub the blood from her legs. By the time the doctor called back, her thighs were raw, but his calm instructions helped her regain her focus. They were going to do an ultrasound to check the baby. If by some small miracle she wasn't miscarrying, then she promised she would put its safety before anything else.

And if that meant ending things with Dan, then so be it.

***

Techno music blasted through the OR, but Dan was too focused on the screen in front of him to pay much attention to the lyrics. The throbbing beat helped him zone out distractions during surgeries and focus on precisely guiding his equipment. He maneuvered the robotic arm holding a pair of tiny scissors between the two metal clamps he'd placed seconds before and cut the neck of the gallbladder. A moment later, he pulled the dark green pouch out through the port. "Come to papa, you bad boy."

His nurse placed it in a formalin jar to go to pathology, and he turned to the anesthesiologist. "What's the time?"

"Fifty-eight minutes."

Dan pumped his fist. "Oh, yeah! New record."

He panned the tiny camera around the abdominal cavity, checking for signs of bleeding and loose clamps. Everything looked stable and secure. "Time to close up shop."

One by one, he removed the instruments and deflated the patient's belly before stitching the peritoneum closed. His brothers had always teased him about his addiction to PlayStation when they were kids, but now those video game skills were paying off. He was one of the few surgeons at the hospital who was trained to perform robotic surgery. To him, it was the ultimate game. The precision, the dexterity, the melding of skill and technology. The reason he'd decided to become a surgeon.

He tied his last stitch and then swapped out the needle driver for a skin stapler. A minute later, the patient was ready to go. "How much time do I have before she wakes up?"

"I'd say at least an hour before she's coherent," the anesthesiologist replied.

"Sounds good. I'll let her husband know we're done, and then swing by radiology to check on my next case."

He grabbed the photos he'd taken of the stone-laden gallbladder to show to the patient and her husband, gave his brief talk to the family in the waiting room to let them know everything went well, and then headed downstairs to pay a visit to the radiologists. Aka, the Shadow Merchants. He'd been consulted on an internal medicine patient this morning due to worsening diverticulitis and had ordered a CT to confirm his suspicions that the guy had a perforated gut. If his estimates were correct, the patient should just be wrapping the study.

The radiologist, Kai, was just beginning a dictation on an ultrasound when Dan stepped into the dark office with multiple computer screens. He lingered in the doorway, not wanting to interrupt while his fellow doctor spoke into the microphone. If he'd learned one thing during his years of medical training, it was "Don't piss off the Shadow Merchants."

"First trimester pelvic ultrasound for patient Hue Jenny Nguyen," the radiologist said in a flat voice.

Dan's chest tightened, making it almost impossible to breathe. His head swam, and he grabbed the door frame to steady himself before he suffered a bout of vasovagal syncope and hit the floor.

Not my Jenny.

Kai continued with his dictation, completely oblivious to him. Dan strained to catch the details as he rattled them off. Single intrauterine pregnancy. Average heart rate of one hundred and fifty six beats per minute. Crown rump length of two point one two inches. Low-lying anterior placenta without evidence of previa or abruption. Estimated gestation age of twelve weeks and five days.

He slumped against the doorway and struggled to catch his breath. Twelve weeks. He calculated backward and put the date of conception to the week of Comic-Con.

FUCK!

I knew I shouldn't have given in to temptation and used that condom, but I thought she was on the pill.

83

Cold sweat pricked his cheeks when he realized she'd never confirmed that one way or another. She'd just nodded when he told her to get some Plan B.

But I pulled out in time.

One glance at the ultrasound screen told him he hadn't.

Fuck, fuck, fuck…

"Dan, are you okay?"

Kai's voice pulled him from the closing walls of panic. "Huh?"

"You look pale. Is everything all right?"

Dan glanced at the ultrasound screen one more time and saw the tiny little fetus frozen in time. A baby.

His baby.

I'm screwed.

He swallowed hard and tried to pull himself together before the whole hospital learned he was about to become a father. He grabbed the empty desk chair and sat down. "Yeah, just a little low blood sugar," he lied. "Haven't had time to eat lunch yet."

"You should grab a bite when you get a chance." Kai turned to the screen to his left and clicked on his patient's name. "It looks like Mr. Ghatak's CT is done."

Dan's hands shook as he forced himself to focus on his patient's findings. His job was to save lives, and the perforated colon found on the CT could kill his patient if he didn't take care of it immediately. He'd deal with Jenny after he'd had time for the news to sink in.

And maybe after he'd had a chance to run this by Adam. If there was ever a time for some big brotherly advice, it was now.

***

Jenny wrapped the coarse woven blanket around her shoulders and waited for the ER doctor to return with her ultrasound report. She'd heard the baby's heartbeat, which had eased some of her anxiety. The baby was still alive. The question was, would it stay alive?

An hour after she'd returned from radiology, he pulled back the curtain and came into her room. "Good news. It doesn't look like you're miscarrying."

Relief flooded through her like rain after a long drought. "But the bleeding this morning?"

"You said there was no cramping, so that made a miscarriage less likely."

"But you don't know the cause?"

"You mentioned that you'd had intercourse this morning, so that was probably the cause. If I were you, I'd hold off on the sex until your OB says it's safe to resume it."

She nodded. *It was my fault. My own selfish fault.*

She hugged her lower stomach, grateful that she hadn't lost the baby.

"Other than that, I'd say you're good to get dressed and go. My nurse will be back in a few minutes with your discharge paperwork. Remember, no intercourse until cleared by your OB."

"I won't forget."

She pulled out her phone and slowly typed out a text to Dan.

It was fun while it lasted, but I think it's time to end our arrangement.

As great as the sex was, it wasn't worth endangering the life inside her.

And as the heavy sensation of mourning filled her, she realized it was better this way. She'd already teetered too close to falling for Dan. Better to make a clean break now than lose both her baby and her heart.

Chapter Eight

Dan dialed Jenny's number and counted the rings before it went to voicemail.

Two.

She'd rejected his call yet again. He let out a curse and resisted the urge to throw his phone across his office. The late afternoon sunlight filtered through the amber leaves on the trees outside his window, bathing the walls in a golden light, but his mood was too dark for him to enjoy it.

Four days had passed since he'd discovered Jenny was pregnant. Four days since she'd sent him the cryptic text message ending their arrangement and shut him out completely. Four days since his world was turned upside down.

It was nothing short of a miracle that he'd made it to Friday without losing his mind. As it was, he wasn't eating, wasn't sleeping, and could barely think about anything else but that little blob of life on the ultrasound screen.

He paced behind his desk, his gut churning. Everything about this situation had him on edge. He was used to being in control, used to calling the shots, used to dictating when things were over. But now the power had shifted to the one woman who wanted nothing to do with him.

Asking Adam for advice would mean exposing his mistake, but he couldn't think of anything else to do at this point. He dialed his eldest brother's number.

Instead of going to voicemail, Adam answered on the second ring. "Hey, Dan."

The churning in his stomach ceased and dropped like a lead weight. "Got a moment?"

"Sure. What's going on?"

Dan ran his finger along the collar of his neatly pressed button-down shirt. Even though his life was going to hell in a hand basket, at least his dry cleaners kept him from looking that way. "Promise not to say a word of this to Mom."

A heavy pause filled the line, followed by, "Tell me what happened."

In his mind, he was prepared to say he'd knocked a girl up, but when he opened his mouth, what came out instead was, "I'm going to be a father."

The air whooshed out of his lungs with his confession, followed by an inability to draw in the next breath. His mind whirled, the world around him teetering in a nauseating form of vertigo. He sank down in his chair before he crashed, pinched the bridge of his nose, and repeated, "I'm going to be a father."

Suddenly, it dawned on him that this was about more than losing Jenny. This was about the baby.

His baby.

Even if Jenny wanted to end things, that still didn't change the fact that the child she carried was his. The possessive urge wiped away the doubt and anxiety and helped him make sense of the chaotic cloud that had surrounded him since Monday. More than anything else, he wanted this child, and he'd do anything to keep it.

"I see," Adam said at last. "And the mother?"

"Is not speaking to me at the moment. Hence, why I called you."

"Why can't my brothers ever come to me with simple problems?" Adam muttered. "Okay, start from the beginning."

"I met Jenny at Comic-Con in July. We had a little one-night fling, but right before she left, we had sex using the emergency condom Caleb slipped me before he deployed, and it broke."

"You're a doctor, Dan. You should know better."

"The wrapper was still intact, and I thought I pulled out in time."

Some incomprehensible sounds came from his brother. Dan could picture Adam sitting with his elbows on his desk, raking his fingers up the hair along his temples the way their father had when they'd done something stupid as kids, and struggling to find something to say other than "You're an idiot."

"How did she find you to deliver this joyous news?"

"She's in Paul's gaming group."

"I thought you swore off gamer chicks."

Dan stared out the window at the gorgeous October day, searching for a dark cloud and finding none. "I had until I met her."

"So you like her?"

"Yes." And until Monday, he could've sworn she felt

the same way.

"And how did you react when she gave you the news?"

"Funny you should ask that." He twirled around in his chair, his back to the window. "She hasn't officially told me yet."

"Then how do you know?"

Sweat prickled the back of his neck, and he rubbed it away before it dampened his collar. "Um, I sort of accidentally saw her ultrasound on Monday."

"And you're sure it was hers?"

"Pretty sure. I even matched the date of conception to Comic-Con."

More incomprehensible muttering. "And yet she's not speaking to you? Why? Did you say something to her about never wanting kids?"

"No. When I ran into her again up here, I even asked her out, but she turned me down. Said the timing was bad and that she couldn't get involved with anyone. But I continued to work on her, and the next thing I knew, she called me up four weeks ago to set up a friends with benefits arrangement. I thought I was finally making some headway until she sent me a text on Monday telling me we needed to end things. Now she won't return my calls or answer my texts, and I'm at a complete loss trying to figure out what to do next."

"Don't you find it a little odd that the day she breaks off things with you was the day you found out she was pregnant? Maybe she's not returning your calls for a reason."

The lead weight in his gut doubled in size, pushing the contents of his stomach into his throat. "What are you talking about, Adam?"

"What if she just found out she was pregnant on Monday and is trying to keep you from finding out about it until she decides whether or not to continue the pregnancy?"

His fingers turned to ice, and his breath shook. "Jenny wouldn't have an abortion."

"You said it yourself—she turned you down because she couldn't get involved with anyone. How do you think a baby is going to fit into her life?"

Despite the chill in his blood, sweat dripped from his hairline. What if Adam was right? What if Jenny was planning on terminating the pregnancy and ended things with him before he found out? What if he had the child taken away from him before he even had a chance to tell Jenny how he felt about it?

A calm, rational voice in the back of his mind told him it was probably for the best. After all, he barely knew her. And he was finally at a point in his life when he could go out and have fun, not be changing diapers and fixing bottles. Did he really want to be saddled with a child when he could be going out and partying, taking home a hot chick every night and never risking his heart again on someone who could break it?

The churning in his stomach returned with a vengeance, requiring several deep breaths before he could say, "I can't let that happen. I want this baby. And I want her."

"Then it sounds like you need to be telling her this, not me."

"But how, when she keeps rejecting my calls?"

"Do you know where she lives?"

"Yes." He drawled out the word, wondering why he hadn't thought of this before.

"Then I suggest you go over there tonight and don't leave until she's heard what you have to say."

"Good idea." He grabbed his coat and headed for the door, determined to be at her place the moment she came home from work. And if that failed, then he'd have to track her down at her office. He wasn't going to risk losing what mattered to him any longer.

He was about to hang up when Adam added, "Oh, and congratulations."

Dan slid to a stop, letting the final word sink in. "Thanks, Adam. But remember, not a word of this to Mom. I'll break the news to her when I'm ready."

"Not a word, but you'd better tell her soon. She keeps harping on me and Lia for a grandchild, and we're not there yet."

Dan doubted it was from lack of trying. Adam adored his wife, and they both wanted to start a family. For their sake, he hoped they wouldn't have to wait much longer. Out of all his brothers, Adam would make the ideal father. "Want me to take pressure off of you, huh?"

"Just think how happy it would make her."

Dan chuckled as he locked up his office. "Once she forgives me for knocking up a girl I wasn't married to."

"She will. Eventually. Once she's chewed you out for a month or so."

"Gee, thanks."

"No problem, little bro. Good luck."

"Thanks," Dan replied just before he hung up and got

into his car. *I'm going to need it.*

***

Jenny climbed the flight of stairs to her condo, hanging onto the railing with each step and cursing the fact her brother had talked her into wearing heels to dinner tonight. The balls of her feet throbbed, and her toes felt like they'd been jammed into a medieval torture device. The ache in her lower back only added to her misery.

Great, it's only the beginning of my second trimester, and I'm already wanting to wear nothing but muumuus and bunny slippers.

But since Mike and Jason wanted to take her out to celebrate that milestone, she'd grudgingly dressed up for the occasion.

When she got to the top of the stairs, though, she forgot about her aches and pains and froze.

Sitting in front of her door with his knees drawn up and his forehead resting on them was Dan.

Her hand flew to her stomach before she realized it, and the fabulous dinner she'd had at Canlis threatened to come back up. "What are you doing here?"

He popped his head up and met her gaze. The haunted expression in his eyes tore at her heart and made her hate what she'd done to him. "I'm waiting for you."

She blinked away the tears that stung the corners of her eyes and reached around him to unlock her door. "Dan, please, I thought I made it quite clear that what we had was just temporary and—"

He silenced her by covering her hand with his. His hair was standing up on end, and deep wrinkles creased his normally stiffly pressed shirt. He looked like he'd been sitting there for hours. "I need to talk to you."

The rapid thudding of her heart shook her whole body, rattling her keys. He wrapped her fingers around her palm, instantly silencing them and sending a calm wave of warmth up her arm to combat the cold dread that stirred inside her chest. If she lingered here any longer, she'd only give into him and end up getting hurt. "We've said enough."

"I'm not leaving until you hear what I have to say."

Out of the corner of her eye, she spied her neighbor watching them through the blinds. No doubt, Mrs. Bennett was waiting for the perfect moment to call the cops, the old busybody.

Jenny's shoulders slumped in defeat. As much as she feared being alone with Dan, she feared having to explain this scene to the homeowners association if the police showed up. "Fine, but only for a few minutes."

"That's all I need." He kept his gaze locked with hers as he entered the condo, the stubborn set of his jaw letting her know he wasn't backing down.

She followed him inside and kicked off her shoes. "Why are you determined to make a mess of things?"

"I could ask you the same thing."

A lump of regret formed in her throat, but she pushed it down. She had to end this now. Even though her OB had reassured her that the quickie on Monday morning hadn't hurt the baby and that it was safe to resume normal activities, she was still an emotional wreck from the stress the scare had given her. That, combined with the fact she was entering her second trimester and probably wouldn't be able to keep her pregnancy a secret much longer, gave her strength to push him away. "Dan, I've told you from the beginning that I can't get involved with anyone."

"But we have something good together, Jenny." He closed the space between them and stroked her cheek. "Please don't call it quits before we even give *us* a chance."

The pleading on his face tested her resolve, forcing her to turn away from him. "There can't be an *us*, Dan."

"Why not? Are you saying that we have nothing in common? Because I can name a dozen things we've stayed up until the wee hours of the morning talking about."

Don't listen to him. Just remember how Duong reacted when he learned about the baby. Remember how much it hurt then, and he was a stranger. You didn't know him like you know Dan. Jenny wrapped her arms around her stomach and squeezed.

When she didn't answer, he continued, "Are you saying that we're not good in bed together? Because I can remember the other morning when you couldn't seem to get enough of me and dragged me back to bed."

Her skin grew hot from the memory of lying in his arms as he moved inside her, from the rush of pleasure that followed when she came. They were more than compatible in the bedroom—she'd never deny that. In fact, they were dangerously compatible, more like fire and dynamite. And *explosive* would be the only word she could think of to describe sex with him.

He moved behind her and brushed her hair to the side, exposing her neck to his warm breath as he said, "Or are you saying there can't be an *us* because you're scared?"

Her chin quivered from the effort required to keep her mouth shut and not tell him he was as accurate as Luke Skywalker's shot into the thermal exhaust port of the Death Star.

"Because you don't have to be scared, Jenny. I'm right here."

But will you be once you learn the truth?

This would hurt more than ripping a Band Aid off sunburned skin, but it had to be done. She turned around, faced him, and said, "I'm pregnant."

She expected him to respond with the same shocked silence as her mother or the disgusted sneer Duong wore when she made the same announcement, but he simply nodded. "I know."

Now she was the one left wearing the slack-jawed expression of pure shock. "How?"

He looked away and rubbed the back of his head, his ears turning pink. "I am a doctor, you know."

"And you're not running away screaming?" Her pulse fluttered wildly in her ears. This couldn't be real. No, it had to be pregnancy-induced hallucination made all the more potent by the overly rich meal she'd stuffed herself with for dinner. And even though she hadn't touched the wine that was served with each course, she still bordered on a drunken high.

He snapped his gaze back to her, his eyes glittering with a fury that sent shivers down her spine. "What kind of man do you take me for?"

"I didn't mean to imply you, Dan, but I—I mean…" She chewed her bottom lip and stared at the fresh mallard green polish on her toes. "What if I told you it wasn't yours?"

"Are you saying you hooked up with other guys at Comic-Con?"

"No, but—"

He shushed her by placing his finger on her mouth. "Then it's not an issue. Besides, baby or no baby, all I really want is you."

"It's hard enough to date someone who isn't hormonal and puking. Are you sure you want to get involved with someone like me?"

He tilted her chin up and ran his thumb along her bottom lip. "I know what I'm getting myself into, and I think you're worth it."

She wondered if she was dreaming it all until his lips met hers. Their previous kisses had been made of pure passion, more part of the foreplay than anything else. They were meant to tease and inflame, to share their hunger for the other person until they reached the frenzy of release. This kiss was different. It was tender and gentle, pleading and worshipful. It embodied everything he'd just told her. He knew she was pregnant, and yet he still wanted her.

She wrapped her arms around his neck and allowed him to deepen the kiss. The familiar warmth of desire flowed through her, but it was more like the steady Seattle rain than a raging torrent. This was a kiss meant to be savored on its own merit and not as a prequel to mattress acrobatics.

Of course, a round of mattress acrobatics wouldn't be so bad, either.

His breath stuttered as he ended the kiss and pulled away, evidence that he was trying to keep his desire in check. But his hands still circled her waist, still held her close to him.

Jenny stroked his cheek and studied him. Her fears faded with every second she stood in his arms. She'd almost made a huge mistake, but thankfully, she'd been given a second chance. "I'm sorry I tried to push you away, Dan. I was scared you'd want nothing to do with me once you found out I was pregnant, but I was wrong." She lowered her eyes and added, "Do you forgive me?"

"Yes." The single word was raw and choked with emotion, but it drew her closer to him than any physical act.

She glanced back up, saw the fire in his eyes, and kissed him in a fierce manner that said far more than she could ever put into words. She wanted him more than ever. She needed to feel him inside her, to join together in a way that only lovers could. With their lips still locked, she tugged his shirt out from his pants and fumbled for the buttons.

Dan responded with a low growl and unzipped her dress. It fell into a puddle around her ankles, followed by her bra, and he lifted her up into his arms to carry her into the bedroom. They tumbled onto the mattress, their tongues never missing a single beat in their erotic dance.

But then Dan changed the rhythm. He broke away and lay on his side next her, staring at her in wonder, but never saying a word. He ran his hand along her cheek, down her neck and shoulder, finally coming to a stop to cup one of her achingly full breasts. Her nipples hardened from the whisper-soft brush of his thumb. He took that as an invitation to draw the taut peak into his mouth, teasing it with this teeth and tongue until she cried out.

Then he dragged his mouth lower, kissing the underside of her breasts while his hands roamed the growing roundness of her stomach.

Jenny dug her hands into the covers to keep from stopping him. Part of her wanted him to go lower, but a prickle of self-conscious fear streaked down her spine. And yet the curiosity, the need, the want kept her from covering up and backing away. The pleasurable sensations he awakened with his kisses far outweighed the doubts that formed in the back of her mind. He worshipped her body like she was a goddess. And by the time he reached her panties, she was all too ready to strip them off for him.

Dan lifted his eyes, his impish smile daring her to give him permission to continue.

She nodded, not knowing what to expect. None of her previous lovers had ever wanted to taste her like this, to tease and torment her sex with their tongues rather than their dicks. But Dan slipped off her panties with well-practiced ease and slid her to the edge of the bed where he waited on his knees.

He touched her with his hands first, opening her up with a sensual massage along her inner thighs. Then he ran his finger along her seam. A shiver of delight raced up her spine from the light touch, and she eagerly awaited what he had in store for her.

He slipped his fingers inside, stroking her slick inner walls while his thumb sought out her clit. A moan broke free from her lips when he found it. This was all mere foreplay, and yet he already had her on the brink of coming.

His grin widened as he pumped his fingers inside, mimicking the motions of his cock. Her hips rolled in response, rising to meet each stroke. She felt wonderfully wanton and yet powerful. She was a woman who deserved pleasure from her lover, and she'd finally found one who knew how to give it to her.

The tension coiled inside her from her approaching release, but just as she was about to climax, he withdrew his hand. A wave of disappointment started to creep over her until he lowered his face between her legs and flicked his tongue along the places his fingers had just been. She gasped when he nipped her clit and exhaled in another moan of ecstasy as he drew it into his mouth, sucking ever so gently on the sensitive bit of flesh. His tongue followed, swirling around it in slow circles.

But as the seconds slipped by, the tempo changed. He pulled her deeper between his lips. The lazy circles turned into frenzied flicks, and before she knew what was happening, she was coming. The exhilarating rush revived her weary body and set her skin on fire. She laced her fingers through his hair, holding him between her legs, begging him not to stop.

But as she came back down from her high, she was vaguely aware of him pulling her back to the pillows and crawling into the bed next to her. The prickle of his chest hair against her arm let her know he'd shed his shirt, and when she lowered her hand, she found his cock straining against the confines of his underwear. She wrapped her fingers around his hard length.

Dear God, she needed him inside her.

Amusement flickered across his face, followed by a tightening of pain. "Please, Jenny," he whispered.

"I'm the one who should be begging." She stripped away his underwear, and he moved on top of her, reaching for the drawer where she kept the condoms.

He pulled one out and paused. "Do you want me to use this?"

Heat flooded her cheeks. He was putting the decision on her. It was a moment where she had to decide if she trusted him completely. "You're clean. I'm clean, and I'm already pregnant, so…"

A huge grin appeared on his face, and he tossed the condom back on the nightstand. "Good, because you felt so wonderful that morning at Comic-Con."

He slid into her, and she understood what he meant. Sex had always been great with him, but the sensation of skin on skin awakened a heightened level of intimacy she enjoyed.

He made love to her slowly, his strokes steady and even while his lips sought hers in a flurry of kisses. She closed her eyes when their lips were joined, focusing on the feeling of him inside, the masculine scent of his skin, the soft purr of contentment that rumbled through his chest from time to time. But every time he ended a kiss, she opened her eyes to find him staring down at her. And when he smiled, she couldn't help but smile back.

For the first time in her life, she held out the hope that someone could love her for herself, and it made the bliss of coming in his arms more intense than any orgasm she'd experienced. A warm glow filled her from the inside and radiated through her skin. It made her heart race and her breath catch before she surrendered completely to it and let the lines between her and Dan blur together.

He came with one final, powerful thrust and collapsed. Shudders wracked his body, yet he managed to keep his forehead pressed against hers, their bodies joined from tip to toe, until he managed to utter, "Wow."

"My thoughts exactly," she replied.

He propped himself up on his elbow and gave her a crooked, satisfied grin. "So, do you think it's safe to tell people we're dating now?"

She laughed in spite of herself. All this time, she'd been trying to convince herself that it was just sex with Dan, but now that she looked back at the last month, they had been dating, even though she'd fought to not call it that. Through the midnight conversations to early dawn sex, she'd grown closer to Dan than anyone else she'd ever dated.

"Yes, I think it's safe to tell people that."

"Good, because I don't think I'd be able to keep us a secret much longer." He kissed her once more with same tenderness as the first kiss that evening and ended by caressing her cheek. "I'm lucky to have found you, and I don't need to ask my lucky die to confirm that."

Her pulse quickened, and she covered his hand with her own. "I could say the same goes for me."

He rolled onto his side, taking her with him, and wrapped his arm around her shoulders.

She lay there, unable to fully relax until she revealed the truth about the baby. "Dan, I was already pregnant when I met you," she whispered against his chest.

"I don't care," he mumbled back in a sleepy voice as he tightened his arms around her.

He didn't ask her anything more about the baby, and she was grateful for that. She'd tell him more about the surrogacy later. No need to rock the boat too much in one night. Right now, all that mattered was that he knew she was pregnant with someone else's child and still wanted her, and that was enough to calm her worst fears.

Chapter Nine

"Whoa! Look out!" Dan jumped between Jenny and the rambunctious Lab that galloped toward the tennis ball that had landed behind them. Visions of Jenny being knocked to the ground and trampled filled his mind. Every fiber of his being screamed that he had to protect her and his baby from the eighty-pound dog that was on a collision course with them. He grabbed her hand and spun her out of the way just as the dog raced past them, leaving splatters of mud in his wake.

Once the danger had passed, anger replaced his panic. How dare the dog's owner throw the ball in their direction? Couldn't he see that Jenny was pregnant?

He shook the mud from his hands and turned to glare at the dog's owner, only to see a man and young boy jogging toward them.

"Sorry about that," the man said. "Caden got a little too excited and didn't look where he was throwing."

Dan opened his mouth to lecture the man on keeping a closer eye on his son and dog, but Jenny's laughter silenced him.

"It's okay," she said, smiling as though the boy had

104

thrown flowers at her instead of the ball. "Part of the danger of coming too close to the dog park."

Dan wrapped his arm around her waist, holding her close and reassuring himself she was uninjured. When he realized he'd made a big deal out of nothing, his anger ebbed, and he forced a weak smile on his lips. "Hopefully he'll be more careful in the future."

"No question about that." The man ruffled his son's hair before grabbing the ball from the Lab's mouth and hurling it into an empty patch of grass. The dog bolted for it, followed by the father and son.

He watched them go, and a strange urge tugged at his heart. In a few years, that could be him, playing at the dog park with his child. Would he be as laid back as that father? Or would he be like he was now, cautious and fearful?

"Are you all right?" Jenny asked, jerking him from his thoughts.

"I was just worried about you and the baby."

She placed a kiss on his cheek. "I'm not made of glass, you know?"

"No, but you are pregnant." And even if she wasn't, he'd probably feel the same way. Jenny was so small, so delicate in his arms that he worried he'd crush her if he held her too tightly. And yet, even during their roughest sex, she never showed any sign of breaking. "Sorry, just being overprotective."

"It's sweet." She gave him another quick peck and looped her arm though his, indicating she was ready to resume their walk.

The last few days had been cold and rainy, much more

like the weather he'd expected to find when he moved to Seattle. But the weak November sun had finally made appearance through the thick gray clouds, and Jenny jumped at the chance to get out of her condo and take a walk in Marymoor Park. Their path took them along the leash-free dog park, where dozens of pups played in the wet grass with their owners. Memories of the carefree days during his childhood filled his mind as they strolled along.

"Maybe I should get a dog," he mused.

Jenny stopped and turned to him. "What brought that on?"

"I was just thinking back. My brothers and I always had a dog to play with growing up. It's one of the happiest things I can remember."

"Are you saying your childhood wasn't happy?"

He furrowed his brows as he tried to figure out why she'd asked that. "I grew up in the middle of six brothers. It was always loud and crazy, and the dog seemed to fit in with all that."

"I didn't ask about the dog, Dan. I was asking about you."

He stared at his hands, opening and closing them into fists, trying to decide if he should reveal that part of his past with her. "I didn't have a typical childhood."

"With six brothers, I can only imagine." She tried to sound light-hearted, but her dark eyes held hints of worry.

"Don't look at me that way, Jenny. There was nothing traumatic." He started walking again, his nerves rattled by how well she was beginning to read him. "What I was trying to say is that I skipped several grades in school and sometimes I wonder if I missed out on some of the typical childhood experiences. I didn't go to my senior prom because I wasn't old enough to drive. I was sixteen when I graduated from high school and nineteen when I graduated from college. I wasn't even old enough to drink when I started med school. I grew up feeling kind of isolated because of that, but I always had my brothers, my gaming buddies, and my dog."

She nodded and stared straight ahead, but the softness around her eyes and the way she pursed her lips told him she understood what he'd gone through growing up far better than any of the bimbos he'd dated over the years. She'd mentioned that she was shy and awkward, but she was also brilliant. He'd stopped by her office several times in the last month and seen the robots she was working on. They were breathtakingly advanced, and yet beautifully harmonious, much like the woman at his side.

"So why don't you have a dog now?" she asked.

"I've been too busy. Med school and residency don't allow you to give a dog the attention it deserves."

"But you're done with those things now."

"Hence the reason why I was musing about getting another one." He pointed to a frisky husky that leapt in the air to snag a Frisbee. "I probably shouldn't get one like that. It wouldn't like being cooped up in the apartment all day."

She shook her head and grinned. "And somehow, I don't see you as the Chihuahua type."

He shuddered at the thought of a little yappy dog. "Absolutely not. Maybe something calm and lazy, like a basset hound."

"I hear they can be noisy when you're not at home."

"Ah, I didn't think about that." He continued for a few more steps before saying, "Maybe I should get a Great Pyrenees like my mom's dog."

"What kind of breed is that?"

"Big, white, furry. Playful, but protective. Gentle, but big enough to make people think twice about breaking into your house." He chuckled as he thought about all the trouble Jasper had given his mom.

"Sounds like a great dog. I'd love to see one in person."

"Maybe you can." He reached into his pocket and squeezed his lucky die, relieved to have finally found a moment to bring up meeting his family without sounding too obvious. "What are you doing for Thanksgiving?"

"Probably sitting at home, watching the Macy's parade on TV while scouring the ads for Black Friday specials."

"You're not celebrating with your family?" he asked, the tension between his shoulder blades easing. He'd been so worried he'd have to convince her to come with him, but it looked like it would be a slam dunk.

Jenny shook her head with a grin. "My mom tried to cook a traditional Thanksgiving dinner about twenty years ago, but the turkey was so tough, you'd think she'd cooked it using a flesh to stone spell. Besides, Jason will be doing Thanksgiving with his in-laws, so we'll probably just end up going to the casino for the buffet."

"Then maybe you can join my family for Thanksgiving up at my brother's place in Vancouver."

Jenny halted, her breath quickening. "Are you sure we're ready for that? Meeting the family? I mean, we've only officially been dating for a month and—"

He silenced her with a kiss. "You're cute when you're

panicked."

"I have reason to panic." She squeezed his hand, her fingers icy against his palm. "What if your family doesn't like me?"

"I can't think of any reason why they wouldn't." Lord knows, he was crazy about her. She was smart, pretty, funny, sexy, and yet still a geek at heart like him.

"I'm not the most outgoing person, and I'm a bit of a geek."

He rubbed her fingers between his palms to warm them. "So am I."

"I'm Vietnamese."

"They won't have a problem with that."

"I'm pregnant." She leveled her gaze with him as she said it, letting him know that was the one thing that worried her the most.

It was also the one thing that worried him. Only Adam knew she was pregnant. He hadn't told anyone else. Hell, as far as he knew, not even Paul knew she was pregnant, and he was both her boss and their mutual friend. But the baby was the one thing that drove him to take this step so quickly. He wanted her to meet his family before the baby was born, to know what kind of family their child would be a part of. Even if things didn't work out between Jenny and him, he was determined to be a permanent fixture in his child's life.

He laced his fingers through hers and closed the space between them. "I won't lie to you, Jenny. It might make things awkward at first, but once they get to know you, I'm positive they'll adore you as much as I do."

"Taking me home to meet your mother and brothers is

a big deal. Are you sure you're ready to take that step with me?"

He wanted nothing more than to erase the worry that filled her dark brown eyes, but he could see why it was there. Part of him shared that worry. The last girl he'd taken home to meet his mother was Cait, and that was only after they'd been dating for two years. But with Jenny, it was different. Yes, they'd only known each other for four months, but he felt a closeness to her that he'd never experienced with any other woman. It was like Jenny knew his soul, possibly because her soul was cut from the same material as his.

He cupped her cheeks in his hands and pressed his nose to hers. "I couldn't be more sure."

Her lips twitched, hesitant at first before blooming into a full smile.

"Besides, it won't be the whole family. Just my mom, two of my brothers, and my sister-in-law. We can save the crazy, full family get-together for another time."

"Thank you." She closed her eyes and rested her head on his shoulder.

He wrapped his arms around her and held her close, fully aware of how quickly he was falling in love with her.

Chapter Ten

Jenny smoothed the wrinkles out of the high-waisted trench coat that thankfully concealed her growing bump and stared out the window at the Vancouver skyline. The frantic fluttering of her heart vibrated through her entire body. Her fingers trembled. And in the back of her mind, a little voice kept asking, *What if they hate me?*

Dan reached over and squeezed her hand, his eyes never leaving the road while he drove. "Relax, Jenny. You have nothing to worry about. It's just Thanksgiving dinner."

Easy for him to say. He wasn't the one who'd be faced with answering the awkward questions about the baby. She was twenty-one weeks today and far past the point where she could hide it under her normal clothes. On Monday, she was planning on biting the bullet and telling Paul when she put in her request for two weeks of maternity leave, but that would be a breeze compared to the prospect of explaining her pregnancy to her boyfriend's family, especially considering it was another man's child.

A tiny kick to her gut reminded her she still hadn't

111

explained the surrogacy to Dan yet. Of course, he hadn't asked her about it, either. It seemed like he'd just accepted she was already pregnant when they met and seemed content with it. Instead, he focused more on her than the baby. The last two months had been just like any other typical dating couple's. He took her out to dinner. He curled up on the couch next to her on the weekends to glom entire seasons of *The Next Generation* or the *Lord of the Rings* trilogy. He took his time making love to her every night and then holding her in his arms afterward. It was almost as though he was ignoring the fact she was pregnant and moving forward as he would with any other woman.

Except now he was taking her to meet his mother. According to Paul, the last time Dan had done that was back in college. And that relationship hadn't ended well.

She threaded her fingers through Dan's and let their calm strength ease the sickening swirling in her stomach. It was just his mom and two of his brothers. It was just a holiday dinner and an overnight stay. They'd be leaving the next day, so it was nothing to worry about.

Easier said than done.

A light drizzle fell over Vancouver, blurring the Canadian waterfront from view as they drove west through the city to a well-to-do residential neighborhood, finally turning into the driveway of a large brick home. The chill in the late November air mingled with her fear and sent a shiver coursing down her spine.

Dan turned to her, worry etched in the lines of his forehead. "Stay inside until I can bring the umbrella around. I want you to stay dry."

The garage door opened, and Dan grabbed her suitcase. "Right on time," he said with a grin.

Jenny offered a quick prayer to whatever god was listening that this first introduction would be smoother than the one time he'd met her family.

She studied the man coming toward them. He was bigger than Dan, maybe three or four inches taller with broad shoulders and well-muscled arms. His hair was as black as hers, and his eyes were more gray than blue. But when he smiled, she could see the family resemblance. The brothers hugged before coming toward her door.

Dan opened it and helped her out. "Jenny, this is my brother Ben."

She tried to keep her voice from shaking as she said, "Nice to meet you, Ben."

"Same here. I was a little surprised when Dan told me he was bringing his girlfriend, but I'm glad you decided to come." He shook her hand. "Sorry the visit has to be so short, but I have to play in Ottawa tomorrow."

"It's fine. I'm on call this weekend anyway." Dan glanced back at her. "Ben plays for the Whales."

He said it like she was supposed to know what he meant. "The Whales?"

Ben laughed, but without any hint of mocking. "I take it you're not a hockey fan?"

She shook her head, wishing she was smaller than she already felt in his presence.

His eyes crinkled in amusement. "I suppose Hailey can give you a quick intro to hockey, then. After all, she's the better player of the two of us."

"Still a bit sore over Sochi, eh?" Dan gave his brother a

113

playful shove.

Ben shook his head. "She may have taken home the gold medal, but I got the only gold that counts." He held up his left hand so the light reflected off his wedding band.

The evident love Ben had for his wife chased away the nervous chill that surrounded Jenny, and her lips rose into a smile. So far, she liked his family. Hopefully, the rest would be as friendly and welcoming as Ben.

"I'll get your things," Ben offered. "Mom's anxious to see you."

Jenny wasn't sure if he meant her or Dan, but it didn't matter once he took her hand. They'd go into the house together.

A low, deep bark greeted them when he opened the door, followed by the galloping thump of paws on hardwood floors. Just like that day in the park three weeks ago, Dan jumped in front of her, shielding her from the approaching dog with his body.

"Jasper, come back here," a woman called from the other room, but that didn't stop the mass of white fur coming toward them.

The dog jumped up in his hind legs, his paws landing on Dan's chest with enough force to make him stumble back a step, and began licking Dan's face.

He laughed and scratched the dog behind his ears. "Good to see you, too, Jasper."

Jasper sniffed the air and turned his soulful dark eyes on her. He jumped down and wove around Dan.

Jenny's muscles tensed, bracing for the same greeting from the massive dog, but instead, he merely sat at her feet, licked her hand, and leaned his head against her stomach.

Jenny ran her hands through the dog's soft fur and smiled. If this was the breed of dog Dan was thinking about getting, she was all for it.

"I've never seen him do that before," the same feminine voice that had called him a minute ago said. A woman with a sleek gray bob stood on the opposite side of the living room and crossed her arms. "Usually Jasper's so excited to see someone, the goofball knocks them down."

"Maybe he knows to be gentle with Jenny." Dan crossed the room and gave the woman a kiss on the cheek. "How are you, Mom?"

"Good as I can be with all of my boys gone," she replied with a heavy note of guilt.

Jenny hid her grin as she started unbuttoning her coat. It seemed her mom wasn't the only one skilled at the guilt trip.

"It's only been four months since I left Chicago." Dan rolled his eyes and held out his hand to Jenny. "Mom, I'd like you to meet my girlfriend, Jenny."

She took a deep breath and hoped she'd make a good first impression. "It's very nice to meet you, Mrs. Kelly."

"The pleasure is all mine." Her warm smile mirrored her sons', and she took Jenny's hand in both of hers, pulling her into a hug.

But the second her bump collided with Mrs. Kelly's stomach, the atmosphere changed. Dan's mother stiffened and pulled away, her hand falling to the obvious bulge hiding under Jenny's dress. Her eyes widened, then narrowed at Dan in accusation.

Jenny's skin grew warm, the flush in her cheeks matching the color she saw creeping into Dan's. She backed away from his mother and moved to his side. It wasn't the first time she'd been the elephant in the room, but the silence grew more nerve-wracking with each passing second.

A tall, blond woman entered the foyer and did a quick survey of the scene before moving between Mrs. Kelly and her and Dan. "Hi, I'm Hailey, Ben's wife. Why don't I take you upstairs so you can freshen up a bit?"

Hailey took the suitcase Ben had just brought in, looped her arm through Jenny's, and dragged her up the stairs before anyone could stop her. It wasn't until they'd reached the landing that she slowed down. "Sorry about that. I figured you needed a little rescuing."

Judging from the muffled conversation coming from below, she'd gotten out just in time. It sounded like Dan was getting the third degree from his mother. "If anyone should be apologizing, it's me. I didn't mean to cause any trouble."

"Don't worry about it." Hailey shrugged and continued down the hallway. "I've been in your position before."

Jenny trailed behind her. "You have?"

"Yeah. It's one thing to explain a pregnancy if you're married, but it's an entirely different situation when you're single."

"You have a child?"

Hailey stopped short, her should blades squeezing together. "Had. Zach passed away a couple of years ago."

A new wave of embarrassment washed over Jenny, but

for an entirely different reason. "Now I'm definitely the one who should be apologizing."

"No need to, Jenny." She gave her a smile that didn't quite chase away the sadness lingering in her eyes. "I've set up this room for you. I hope you like it."

Jenny shrugged off her coat and looked out at the perfectly groomed gardens outside. "It's lovely."

"And Dan will be across the hall," Hailey added with a wink. "Maureen insisted you have separate rooms."

She giggled in spite of herself. Dan had been sleeping over at her place almost every night for the last three months. She doubted she'd be alone for long.

But the sounds of the conversation continuing downstairs chased away her mirth. The baby moved inside her, and her hand reflexively fell to her stomach, even though she knew it was too early to feel the kicks from the outside. "Maybe I should stay up here the rest of the evening. It sounds like Dan hadn't told anyone about me."

"None of us were expecting it, and I have a feeling Maureen just got the shock of her life. But she's not the type to overreact. I'm guessing by the time we go back down, everything will be fine again." Just as the words left Hailey's mouth, the conversation below quieted.

"Maybe, but perhaps I should give them a few more minutes before returning." She decided to change the subject. "Ben mentioned you'd gotten a gold medal."

Hailey stood a little taller, her smile beaming with pride. "Would you like to see it?"

"I'd love to."

***

Dan's pulse pumped through his body as the full wrath

of his mother's icy glare fell on him.

Thankfully, she waited until Hailey had absconded with Jenny before ripping him a new one.

"Daniel Oliver Kelly, you have some explaining to do."

Shit! He hadn't been called by his full name since he was seven. Usually, it was Frank who was getting the third degree from their mom. He'd always been "the smart one," the one who never got into trouble. He was just waiting for his mom to grab him by the ear and drag him to the corner, the way she had when he was little.

But despite the anger simmering in her voice, she didn't raise it above the level of normal conversation.

He retreated until he was backed against the kitchen counter and rubbed the back of his head. "Um, what about, Mom?"

"You know damn good and well what I'm talking about." She closed the space between them, every inch the prosecuting attorney she'd been before she married his dad. "How far along is she?"

He'd been dreading this conversation since the moment he'd found out about the baby, but now that his mom knew, there was no getting around it. He counted back in his mind, wishing he had one of those pregnancy wheels that had gotten him through his OB rotation in med school. "Her due date is April eighth, so that would make twenty weeks and a few days, I believe."

"Twenty weeks? She's already halfway through her pregnancy, and you didn't tell me?"

He looked to Ben for help, but his older brother just grinned and gave a subtle shake of his head, obviously enjoying the show.

Great. I'm in this alone. "If it's any consolation, I just found out a few weeks ago myself."

"What do you mean, you just found out? How long have you been dating her?"

"Define dating."

Even though his mother kept her demeanor quiet and contained, the anger exploding inside manifested in the twitch of her eye and the thinning of her lips. And his response had just tripped her over into the danger zone.

Thankfully, that was when Gideon decided to come in through the back door. His younger brother looked at their mom and let out a low whistle. "Uh-oh, someone's in deep shit."

"Watch your language," their mother snapped, diverting some of her ire toward Gideon, much to Dan's relief.

"Dan decided to bring his pregnant girlfriend to Thanksgiving dinner," Ben said, still wearing that amused grin.

Time to wipe that smirk off his face. "Well, it's not like I'm the first one of us to knock up a girl during what was supposed to be a one-night stand." Dan jerked his head toward Ben.

Ben's grin fell, and an aching look of regret filled his eyes. His son, Zach, had died before he had a chance to know him, and he knew his brother still mourned him.

Dan cussed under his breath. "Sorry, Ben, I shouldn't have gone there."

"But you're right," he replied in a quiet voice. Then he turned to their mother. "Mom, you should at least give Dan some credit for staying with her."

"Exactly, Mom. Trust me when I say that no one was more shocked than me to learn about the baby, but it's my kid, and I want to try and make this work with Jenny. So please, don't do anything to scare her away. She's already nervous about meeting the family, and she doesn't deserve the third degree for my mistake."

His mother blinked several times and backed away, her lips parted in surprise.

"And look on the bright side," Gideon added. "You're finally going to become a grandmother."

The last traces of anger melted from their mother's rigid posture, and she clasped her hands together like an excited child about to receive a present. "That's right."

Dan shot a look of thanks to Gideon.

"So, are you going to marry her?" his mom asked.

His throat tightened, and he coughed to clear it. "Haven't there been enough weddings this year?"

"Daniel." Her voice rose in warning.

"What?" He squirmed under the pressure of her glare. "Just because we're having a kid together doesn't mean we have to get married. This is the twenty-first century, after all."

"I raised you better than that."

"Mom, please, I'd rather not rush into things."

"It's a little late for that."

"Yeah, and lots of couples get married after the baby's born." But his argument seemed to be getting nowhere with his mom, so he took a deep breath and decided to lay it all on the line. "Listen, I know this is a bit out of order, but I really do like Jenny. I think I'm even falling in love with her, so yeah, there's a good chance I'll ask her to marry me. Hell, why do you think I decided to subject her to a holiday with the family? I wanted her to feel comfortable around you and to know she's welcome in the Kelly clan, so please, just give her a chance, get to know her, and please don't do anything to screw things up between us."

His mom stayed silent, patting Jasper on the head while she appeared to mull over his confession. Then she nodded. "I think that's the first smart thing that's come out of your mouth all day."

Jasper woofed and took off for the stairs. Jenny's laugh echoed from the next room over, and a moment later, she reappeared with Hailey. Her dark eyes glowed with excitement. "I got to hold two Olympic medals."

Then she spotted Gideon and paled. Her voice shook as she asked, "What's he doing here?"

Jenny may not have recognized Ben, but there was no way she couldn't have known his young brother. Gideon's face was everywhere.

Dan crossed the room and wrapped his arm around her waist. "Jenny, this is my brother, Gideon."

"Your brother is Gideon Kelly?" Her breath came in shallow pants, and her hand trembled until she took his and squeezed it.

"Smooth, bro." Gideon flashed his famous smile at her. "I thought you'd be dropping my name everywhere to pick up chicks."

"No, that would be Frank's MO," Dan shot back. He hugged Jenny, noting the way her shoulder curled up and her heels remained planted, despite his efforts to bring her closer to his brother. "There's no need to panic," he

121

murmured.

"But he's a movie star," she whispered back.

"He's also my baby brother. I remember him waddling around the house in diapers."

"We all do." Ben ruffled Gideon's dark hair. "Or how he had to wear braces from the time he was eight."

"Yeah, yeah, yeah." Gideon ducked out of Ben's reach. "Bring up every embarrassing thing you can."

"And with seven boys, group baths were a must. I even have pictures I can show you." Their mom turned to leave the room and retrieve the incriminating evidence.

"Don't," all three boys said in unison, freezing her in her tracks.

Giggles bubbled up from Jenny's chest, and she covered her mouth to contain them. The tension fled her muscles as she leaned into him. "Sorry if I seemed a little starstruck, Gideon, but I was expecting Thanksgiving dinner with a normal family, not one filled with celebrities."

"But we are a normal family." Dan's hand grazed the side of her stomach, reminding him why this trip was so important. "Just give us a chance."

She looked up at him and nodded. "I can do that."

"Good." His mother came over and led Jenny away from him. "Hailey and I could use a little help getting dinner on the table. How are you in the kitchen?"

"Awful," she replied with a laugh. "I burn toast."

"Don't worry, Jenny, I'm sure we can find something for you to do." His mom glanced over her shoulder and gave him a wink. "Why don't you boys take Jasper outside and let him run around so he won't try to steal the turkey."

"Yeah, we don't want a repeat of the 2010 Thanksgiving disaster," Gideon said dryly as he opened the door and ushered the dog out.

Dan followed his brothers, looking once more into the kitchen to make sure Jenny was all right before he left her alone. She was smiling and chatting with his mother and Hailey, already at ease with them, and the worry in his gut eased. If everything went well today, then maybe he wouldn't be too far off from popping the question.

Chapter Eleven

Jenny sniffed the garlic mashed potatoes before scooping up a heap and dropping it onto her plate. Her stomach rumbled. The food smelled heavenly. Such a change from a few weeks ago, when every little scent made her queasy. She passed the bowl to Ben and took the gravy from Dan, pouring a generous amount on her turkey and stuffing.

"Hungry?" Dan teased.

"Ravenous." Her mouth had been watering since she'd been recruited to help in the kitchen. Thankfully, that meant very little actual cooking. Maureen and Hailey had done most of the work before they'd arrived. She helped with the last-minute prep work and set the table, relieved that the dinner was playing out normally.

Normal.

She'd forgotten what that word had meant over the past few months.

Once everyone started eating, though, Dan's mom focused her attention on her. "What's your due date, Jenny?"

A paralyzing sense of dread seized her. She lowered her

eyes. "April eighth."

"And do you know what you're having yet?"

The juicy turkey that had tasted so delicious moments ago now felt like sawdust on her tongue. If Maureen kept asking questions about the baby, then she'd eventually have to reveal the whole convoluted story about how she had agreed to be a surrogate for her brother.

"The ultrasound is scheduled for next week," Dan answered. "We'll find out then."

"You'll have to call me as soon as you know."

"Don't worry, Mom, we'll let you know what we're having. No doubt, you're going to spoil your grandchild rotten."

Shit, shit, shit! The word kept playing over and over again in her mind. She'd told him it wasn't his, and he'd said he hadn't cared, but how awake was he when she tried to tell him? Had he even understood what she'd said? Obviously not since he sounded like he thought he'd be raising it like it was.

She had to set things straight. She had to tell him the truth—that the baby would be going to her brother and his husband as soon as it was born—but if she did, would he still want her? Would she be sitting here at the Thanksgiving table with his family if she'd told him about this surrogacy from the beginning?

Guilt squashed what was left of her appetite. She needed to come clean soon, but this wasn't the appropriate time and place. But tomorrow, when they got home, she'd explain everything and hope for the best.

"Just don't spend too much on Dan's baby," Ben said, casting a meaningful glance to Hailey. When she nodded, he continued, "Hailey's due in July."

"Two grandchildren?" Maureen got up from her chair and hugged Hailey. "This is such wonderful news! I'm so happy for the both of you."

"We've been planning on telling you the news over dinner for weeks." Hailey beamed with pure joy, the way Jenny had always imagined an expectant mother would. "And the timing is perfect since the baby will come during the off season."

"Why did you wait to tell us?" Maureen scolded.

"Because so many pregnancies end in miscarriages, and we didn't want to get your hopes up until we knew Hailey was past the first trimester." Ben's eyes softened as he looked at his wife.

Jenny slid her gaze over to Dan to see how he was taking the news. The creased line between his brows vanished as though he'd finally solved a puzzle, and he leaned into her to whisper. "Is that why you didn't tell me at first?"

It was better to lie than to cause a scene, so she nodded.

"Ah, I see now." He covered her hand with his and squeezed it. "Congratulations, Ben and Hailey. It's so great that our kids will be so close in age."

"And only a few hours from each other, too." Maureen circled the table and gave Dan a hug.

Jenny forced a happy smile on her face when Dan's mom did the same to her.

"So, Gideon, do you have any good news to share with us?" Dan teased.

"Yeah," he replied with a deadpan delivery. "I'm going

to be wearing two condoms every time I have sex for the foreseeable future."

The table erupted in laughter, and Maureen came back around the table to give him a playful smack on the back of his head.

Jenny slouched down in her chair and picked at her food through the rest of the meal. As much as she liked Dan's family, she wondered if they'd still want anything to do with her when they learned the baby wasn't his.

***

Dan stood at the bottom of the stairs, indecision warring with the sense of unease that had formed at the base of his spine during dinner. Everything had seemed to be going well, but as soon as the meal was over, Jenny excused herself, saying she needed a nap. He hadn't missed the way she seemed to pull away from the conversation after Ben and Hailey's announcement, or that she'd barely touched the food on her plate.

He took a step up, only to have his mom come up behind him and pull him down. "Let her sleep. It's hard work being pregnant."

"I just want to make sure she's okay. She seemed a little off during dinner."

"She's probably exhausted from the travel and meeting everyone all at once. The turkey probably didn't help, either. Besides, Frank's game is on TV."

He cast one more glance up the stairs before conceding to his mother. After all, she'd had seven kids. She probably knew what she was talking about.

"Boom!" Ben shouted as he came into the living room.

"What did I miss?" his mom asked, running past him

and picking up her glass of chardonnay from the end table.

"Frank just plowed the quarterback into the turf," Ben answered.

His brothers were on the long sectional sofa, beers in hand as they stared at the seventy-two inch TV while Hailey sat on the end with Jasper's head in her lap and flipped through a magazine. His mom took the spot on the other side of the dog, and Ben and Gideon parted to give him enough space to sit.

"That's my boy," his mom said with pride as the camera zoomed in on Frank's cheeky grin.

Dan took the beer Ben offered him and leaned back. The game distracted him from his worries, and he reveled in the time he spent with his family. He'd lived in Chicago his whole life, but he never realized how much he missed them until he moved to Seattle.

When the game turned to a commercial, he nudged Gideon. "Where's Sarah?"

"Red decided to stay in LA," he said, the clipped words telling Dan he didn't want to talk about it now. Probably for a good reason, since Gideon rarely went anywhere without his assistant. He'd been up in Vancouver for the last couple of weeks, crashing in the small carriage house on Ben's property while he worked on a movie.

The game came back on, and at halftime, his mom pulled out her iPad to FaceTime Adam and Lia. Thankfully, Adam revealed nothing when their mom told him about Jenny's pregnancy.

Loud conversations in Italian filled the background, and Adam rolled his eyes at one point. "When Lia said she was inviting her family over for Thanksgiving, I thought she just meant her mom. Instead, she brought over her cousins from Italy, and her Zia Carolina tried to take over the kitchen."

Dan chuckled. Lia was one of the finest chefs in Chicago, and he could only imagine the sparks that would fly if someone tried to usurp her domain. "How much longer are they in town?"

Adam grimaced. "Through Sunday. At least Nick and Giovanni are cool. "

The sound of female voices rose even higher, and Adam glanced over his shoulder. "I'd better go before they start throwing knives. Congrats to everyone. I'll pass on the good news to Lia."

Adam hung up just as the third quarter was getting underway.

Jenny reappeared near the end of the game. Gideon stood and gave her his spot on the sofa, which she silently took.

Dan reached over and stroked her silky black hair, earning a weak smile from her. She curled her legs up under her and leaned her head on his shoulder. "Who's winning?" she asked.

"Atlanta."

Just as he answered, Frank intercepted the ball and ran it back for a touchdown. His family jumped up from their seats, shouting and exchanging high-fives. Jenny, however, stayed where she was, her brow furrowed in confusion.

"Frank's my brother," Dan explained, pointing to the TV screen.

Her eyes widened, and panic washed over her face once

129

again. "Do you have any more famous brothers I should know about?"

"Well, there's Ethan." He turned to his mom. "How is Ethan doing, anyway?"

She shook her head. "He's staying clean, but otherwise, he really doesn't want to talk much. Says he's too busy working on a solo album."

"Ethan was the lead singer for Ravinia's Rejects," he explained, and Jenny turned another shade paler. That name she apparently recognized.

"And your other brothers? Are they astronauts or politicians or something like that?"

"Nah. Adam runs the family business, and my twin, Caleb, is a pilot in the Air Force. Pretty normal stuff." Another commercial came on with twenty-nine seconds left on the clock, but the game was over as far as he was concerned. "What does your brother do?"

"He's a lawyer."

"What kind of lawyer?" his mom asked, leaning forward to snag any details she could about Jenny.

"Environmental law."

"And do you have any other siblings?"

Jenny shook her head. "My mom always said the two of us were enough to drive her insane."

"If she's insane, then I'm probably ready to be committed," his mom joked. She snatched the remote from Ben and turned down the volume. "And what do you do?"

"I'm a robotics engineer," she said slowly, casting a sideways glance to Dan for help.

"Don't look so nervous, Jenny," his mom said. "It's

just that Dan's told us so little about you, and naturally, we want to get to know you better."

Especially since my mom's already assuming we'll be married by this time next year. "Jenny's brilliant. She's working on this robot that can be remotely controlled by just hand movements. No equipment. No joysticks. Just a camera."

"It's nothing that extraordinary," she said, her cheeks flooding with heat.

"Of course it is. What you've developed is so precise, I could perform surgery across the globe with it." His chest filled with pride as he described her project to his family. Jenny chimed in and explained her goals for it, including the ability to perform surgeries from the other side of the world. As she talked about her work, her shyness melted away, and his family could finally see the real Jenny he'd fallen for.

As she was winding down the conversation, Caleb and Alex called using FaceTime to show off the 1968 Chevelle they were restoring. Before long, Jenny and Alex were swimming in engineering jargon, leaving the rest of them in the dust.

Caleb finally had to wrestle the iPad away from his wife. "This is what happens whenever Alex gets around another engineer," he said with a dramatic roll of his eyes.

"Tell Jenny thanks for helping me solve the problem with the transmission," Alex shouted in the background before sliding under the hood of the Chevelle.

They passed his mom's iPad around so everyone could chat with Caleb. Once the call was over, the women got up to reheat some of the leftovers, leaving Dan with his brothers.

"I like her," Ben said, nodding toward the kitchen.

"Me, too." Gideon changed the channel to an NHL game. "She seems like she gets you. Have you shown her your lucky die yet?"

"Yeah, and she's cool with it. She's a total geek like me. I even met her at Comic-Con."

"Ah, so the real story is coming out." Gideon sat down on the ottoman in front of Dan. "So, let me guess. You hooked up with her, knocked her up, and then she tracked you down afterward?"

He wiped his damp palms on his jeans. "Um, not exactly."

Ben handed him a fresh beer from the cooler by the sofa. "Enlighten us."

"Well, the first part is correct. I did hook up with her at Comic-Con. But the kicker was that she's a friend of Paul's and plays in the same D&D game. Talk about an unlikely coincidence. I mean, out of the thousands of women at Comic-Con, what's the likelihood I'd meet one of Paul's gaming buddies there?"

"Sounds like it was meant to be," Gideon said in a high-pitched, quavering voice, before going back to his normal tone. "Seriously, they should make a movie about this."

"Shut up." Dan gave his younger brother a playful shove. "But there may be some truth to that. I mean, what are the odds that I would run into her again? And at a D&D game of all places? All I know is that I was crazy about her before I found out about the baby, and now that I know…"

His voice trailed off when he thought about the

implications. The thought of settling down with one woman used to terrify him, but when he imagined doing it with Jenny, it felt as natural as breathing.

Ben gave him a sympathetic nod, and Gideon braced his arm on Dan's shoulder. "If you need a recommendation on a ring designer, let me know. I'll hook you up like I did Ben."

"Thanks." He shrugged off Gideon's arm. "So, what happened between you and Sarah?"

The mirth left his little brother's face, and he played with the label on his beer bottle. "What makes you think something happened?"

"Because you're here, and she's not."

"I've been meaning to ask the same thing," Ben added.

"You know how we are. I'll say something stupid. She'll get upset, but then in a few weeks, we're back to being friends again. It's been that way for years, guys."

But based on the way Gideon was avoiding the question, there was more to it than just a friendly disagreement. "What did you say to her this time?"

Gideon peeled away the last of the label and gave a huge sigh. "Not a word of this to anyone."

"Geek's honor," Dan replied, holding up his hand in the Vulcan sign.

"We were at a Halloween party, and I got a little wasted, and all I remember was asking her if she'd ever consider being more than friends. And she bristled like a cat whose tail had been stepped on and left the party."

"Did she ever tell you why?" Dan asked.

He shook his head, his eyes still downcast. "She basically avoided me for the next few days and then said she was going to manage things from LA while I was up here. I apologized and told her she was welcome to join us for Thanksgiving, but I think I may have finally crossed the line and really fucked things up between us."

"Did you mean what you said? Or were you just trying to get laid?"

"No, I meant it." Gideon finally looked up from his empty beer bottle. "Hollywood's just so crazy, so fake. Red's the only real person I know down there, and she gets me, you know? But the more I think about it, the more I can see things from her perspective. She's spent the last six years trying to avoid the spotlight, especially after all the shit she went through, and if we started dating, then she'd be right back in the middle of it. The tabloids would have a field day, and I know it's selfish of me to even ask her, but it's something I've always wondered about."

And she'd given her answer loud and clear. After experiencing something similar when Jenny tried to push him away, Dan's heart went out his brother.

Ben retrieved the last beer from the cooler and gave it to Gideon. "Just give her some time, Gid. She'll come around. She always does."

"Yeah, but maybe I should give her a call and check in on her, make sure she's okay." He pulled out his phone and went outside.

They sat in silence for a few minutes before Ben spoke to Dan. "Do you love her?"

"I think so."

"Then don't wait too long to tell her." He glanced out the window where Gideon paced back and forth on the phone. "I'm going to head into the kitchen and grab some more food. You coming?"

"Sure," he replied, still mulling over Ben's advice. His older brother didn't say much, but when he did, it was usually something important. He stood beside Jenny while she ate and joined the conversation with his family, wondering what she'd say if he suggested they get married. Would she say yes? Or would he end up like Gideon, scrambling to hold onto what he already had?

Chapter Twelve

Dan's car was merging onto I-405 toward Seattle's Eastside when Jenny opened her eyes. She'd spent most of the morning on a whirlwind tour of Vancouver with his family, growing more and more aware of the guilt weighing down on her shoulders. They all thought the baby was his and were treating her as though she was already part of the family. Exhaustion claimed her as soon as they got on the road home, and she fell asleep. Now, they were almost back to her place, and she still hadn't found a chance to tell him the baby wouldn't be staying with them.

"Have a good nap?" he asked.

She stretched and yawned. "Too good. I'm sorry I was poor company for the ride back."

"Don't apologize. It gave me time to think."

"About what?"

"Random stuff." He moved into the HOV lane to bypass the traffic. "Mostly that it was time to start looking for a house."

She reached for her water bottle and took a long gulp to ease the nervous dryness in her throat. "Tired of my little condo already?"

"It's nice for now, but it's only one bedroom." His gaze flickered to her stomach.

Unease prickled the skin along her back, and she squirmed in her seat. The implications of his suggestion were coming in loud and clear, and if he wasn't speeding down the freeway, she would've told him right then that they didn't need to make room for the baby because it wasn't theirs.

"I'm open to suggestions," he continued. "What are some of the better neighborhoods around here?"

"They're all pretty good over here."

He squeezed the steering wheel and curled his lips in. "I guess what I'm trying to say is that I'd appreciate your input, Jenny. Whatever I end up buying, I want you to be comfortable there."

"There's really no need to run out and buy a house now, Dan. We're fine with what we have."

"Maybe, but the baby will be here in a few months, and I want to make sure we have room for it."

An ache formed in her chest, so intense it made it hard to breathe. This was her chance to tell him, her moment to set things straight and possibly jeopardize her entire relationship with him. She wiped her hands on her jeans, gathered her strength, opened her mouth to say the words she'd been dreading since she met him.

And then his cell phone rang.

Dan answered it and discussed a case through the Bluetooth with one of his partners. By the time they hung up, they were back at her complex. Jenny climbed up the stairs to her place while Dan grabbed their bags, every beat of her heart demanding she tell him. She unlocked her door only to find Mike sitting on her couch, flipping through the sports channels on her TV.

Time to change the key code on her door. "What are you doing here?" she asked.

"I just wanted to show you what I got on sale today." He stood up and gave her a bear hug. "And how is my little baby mama?"

"Tired and really wishing you weren't here right now."

"Long weekend with the boy's family—I get that." He rested his massive hand on her bump and leaned over to speak to it. "And how's my little bundle of joy? Daddy can't wait to see you and hold you in my arms and spoil you rotten."

Jenny's skin flushed from all the attention Mike was paying to her stomach, but the thump of a suitcase behind her chilled her blood.

" 'Daddy'?" Dan asked in a cold, hollow voice.

Her pulse kicked into overtime, and she slowly turned around.

Dan stood in the doorway, a lethal light in his eyes as he glared at Mike's hand on her bump.

"Well, it *is* my baby," Mike replied nonchalantly, never looking up from her stomach. "What else would I be called?"

Dan's nostrils flared, and his hands balled into fists. His attention shifted her, and fear shook her knees. Out of all the ways for him to find out about the surrogacy, this had to be the worst-case scenario. "Is it his?" he asked.

Mike's head jerked up, and he rose to his full height, challenge written all over his face. He rested one hand on her shoulder in a gesture that was both possessive as well as protective.

Jenny closed her eyes and gave Dan a single nod.

Her front door slammed shut, and heavy footsteps banged down the stairs outside.

She snapped her eyes open and ran after him. "Dan, please, come back!"

But by the time she got outside, he was tearing out of the parking lot in a squeal of tires.

A sob choked her throat as she watched him drive away. It was over. She'd known this day would come from the moment she met him, but there'd always been some part of her that held out the hope that they could make things work. But she'd waited too long, and this was the result.

"Come inside before you catch your death of cold," Mike said softly.

Hot tears fell down her cheeks, but she refused to move from the landing. Maybe he'd turn around and come back. Maybe he just needed to cool off and let the news sink in.

But she yielded when Mike wrapped his arm around her shoulders and led her back inside. He sat her down on the couch and handed her a box of tissues. "Tell me what just happened here."

"He didn't know."

"Didn't know what?"

"That I was acting as your surrogate."

Mike drew in a deep breath through his nostrils and exhaled. "But he knew you were pregnant?"

She nodded and blew her nose.

139

"Did you lie and tell him the baby was his?"

She shook her head. "No. He said he didn't care, but it was just after sex, so he may not have heard me correctly. But I never told him about the surrogacy."

"So you purposely omitted important information in order to deceive your boyfriend? Is that correct?"

She felt pity for anyone on the witness stand when Mike was cross examining them. The man was like a heat-seeking missile when it came to establishing guilt. "I didn't set out to deceive him."

"But by not correcting him, you still lied to him. And I would've reacted the exact same way if I were in his shoes." Mike pressed the heel of his hand to his temple. "Just one more question. Is there any chance the baby could be his?"

Jenny shredded the wet tissue in her hands. "We did have unprotected sex at Comic-Con."

"So there's a chance, right?"

For once, she was glad she'd cracked open that pregnancy handbook her OB had given her and read the first few chapters about conception. "A small one, but I doubt the pregnancy test would've turned positive so quickly if it was his. I mean, it was only a week after we hooked up."

"Jesus," Mike muttered before he sat down next to her. "This isn't like you at all, Jenny."

"I know." She grabbed a fresh tissue and dabbed her eyes, but the tears kept falling. "But it all started out because I wanted to know what I was missing. And when I finally had a taste of it..." She stared at her lap. "You're not going to tell Jason, are you?"

"Are you asking me to lie to my husband?"

"No, just omit certain bits and pieces."

Mike raised one dubious brow. "And we saw how well that worked out for you."

The image of Dan's face when he saw them triggered a new wave of sobbing that bordered on hysterics, yet she couldn't stop it. She hated knowing she'd hurt Dan. She hated seeing the betrayal on his face. And she hated that she'd probably ruined the best thing she'd ever had.

Mike pulled her against his chest and hugged her while she cried into his designer shirt. "Okay, that's enough. Crying won't solve anything."

"I know, but I don't know what else to do. Damn pregnancy hormones."

He chuckled and rubbed her back. "You could probably get a temporary insanity plea with those."

And just like that, her sobs turned to laughter. She lifted her head and wiped the last of her tears away. "Think we can get away with it, counselor?"

"Maybe." He smiled and caught the final tear with his thumb as it streaked down her cheek. "So, time to form a defense strategy. Do you want him back?"

"Yes, I do, but why would he want me?"

Mike wagged his finger. "I won't stand for that kind of negative thinking, Ms. Nguyen. The first step to getting what you want is to believe you deserve it."

"That's the tricky part. It's hard to believe someone like me deserves someone like him. Dan's everything I could've wanted, and you saw how desperate I was to keep him."

"Then let me see what I can do to smooth things over

141

for you." He kissed the top of her head and stood. "But for now, have some tea, watch a movie, and relax. All this worrying is not good for the baby."

"I'll try." But even after Mike left, she replayed the whole confrontation and wondered what she could've done differently. After half an hour, she finally pulled out her phone and dialed Dan's number.

It went straight to voicemail.

She waited for the beep and said, "Dan, I'm sorry. Please, just give me a chance to explain everything." Her breath caught, and she added the one thing she hoped would convince him to call her back. "I love you."

***

Dan dropped his bags at the door of his apartment and went straight for the liquor cabinet. If anything called for a good stiff drink, it was this. He unscrewed the lid from the bottle of Jameson and took a long swing.

How could I have been so stupid?

How could I have fallen for her lies?

God, it was Cait all over again.

He took another gulp and carried the bottle to the sofa. Part of him wanted nothing more than to get completely shitfaced, but a small voice in the back of his mind warned him that he was on call tomorrow, and operating with a hangover was just opening the door for a malpractice suit. So instead of consulting the Jameson, he turned to the next best thing.

His eldest brother.

He dialed Adam's number and breathed a small prayer of thanks when he answered. "Hey, Dan, I just got off the phone with Mom. She kept going on and on about how much she liked Jenny and how—"

"The baby's not mine."

Adam grew silent. "I see. Let me go someplace a little more quiet." A few seconds later, the background conversations vanished. "What do you mean, the baby's not yours?"

"Just that." He took another drink from the bottle. "We got home, and there was this big black man in her place calling her his baby mama and fondling her belly. And when I asked her if it was his, she said yes."

"Shit." The brisk footsteps on the other side of the line told him Adam was pacing. "So, what do you think about this?"

"What do I think? I think I dodged a major bullet. Should've known better than to get involved with another gamer. You'd think I would've learned that lesson from Cait."

"Do you really think Jenny was like her?"

"The evidence is right there. She's pregnant with another man's child and had the gall to make me believe it's mine. The kicker was that he's married. I saw the ring on his hand. What else is she hiding from me?"

More footsteps filled the line. "But based on everything Mom told me, this doesn't sound like the girl you brought up to Ben's. Did you give her a chance to explain?"

"What is there to explain? She confirmed it was his, and that's all I needed to know. She's a two-timing slut like Cait, and I can't believe I was stupid enough to consider marrying her."

"Why were you thinking of marrying her? Was it only because of the baby?"

Dan winced from the fire in his chest that he wished he could blame on the whiskey. Yes, there was a part of him that was disappointed to learn the baby wasn't his. He was actually looking forward to fatherhood, to having a kid of his own. But the deeper cuts came from Jenny's betrayal. He'd fallen so hard for her that this revelation made him question his own judgment.

"No," he replied, his voice raw with pain.

"Then if you really loved her, you should at least hear her side of the story."

"No, I'm not going to be that stupid again, Adam."

"Then why did you call me if you're not going to take my advice?"

Dan stared at the bottle of whiskey and debated if he'd had enough before setting it down on the end table. "I suppose I just wanted someone to know that I'd been a fool."

"The only foolish thing you're doing is jumping to conclusions and potentially walking away from the love of your life."

"There will be others," he said, more to himself than Adam. But he'd learned his lesson. He wouldn't let any of them get close to him again.

"And I always thought you were the smart one."

Adam hung up before Dan could offer a rebuttal.

Chapter Thirteen

"Dr. Kelly," Gayle said as he came out of a patient's room, wringing her hands in worry, "I didn't know what to do, so please don't be upset with me."

"It's hard to be upset when I don't know what's up." Dan bid his final patient of the morning farewell and turned his attention to the receptionist.

She handed him a business card. "This lawyer showed up and said he wouldn't leave until he spoke with you, and I was so worried about him causing a scene in the waiting room that I directed him to your office."

Dan's gut tightened with worry. Anytime a doctor got an unexpected visit from a lawyer, it usually meant bad news. He read the name on the card, noting he listed "Business Litigation" as his specialty. "It's okay, Gayle. You did the right thing. Go take your lunch, and I'll take care of Mr. Warren from here."

His receptionist gave him a cautious nod before retreating to the lunchroom.

He flipped the card over, looking for any clues before making his way down the hall. As far as he knew, he hadn't done anything to warrant a lawsuit.

The instant he saw the black man from Jenny's apartment sitting in his office, the same jealous rage coiled in his muscles. His fingers reflexively curled into his palms, and he struggled to keep his face blank and his voice flat as he greeted him. "Mr. Warren, I presume."

"Dr. Kelly," he replied with a nod and rose from the chair. If the fact he was a litigator wasn't intimidating by itself, the man's sheer presence would be more than enough to make most men watch their words. He was maybe an inch or two taller than Ben, but just as muscular. The quiet intensity burning in his eyes made it very clear he wouldn't leave until he'd had his say, but he still held out his hand and gave him a friendly smile. "Thank you for taking a moment to meet with me."

Dan didn't take his hand, choosing instead to take off his white coat and roll up his shirt sleeves. He needed to put his desk between them before he gave into the barbaric urges brewing inside him. He wanted nothing more than to pound the shit out of the man who'd impregnated Jenny. "You have a lot of gall showing up here after Friday night."

"I'm here on behalf of Jenny." He waited for Dan to sit down before doing the same. "There seems to be a little misunderstanding that I'd like to clear up."

Dan focused on stacking the charts on his desk. "The only misunderstanding here was the fact I was led to believe the child was mine."

"Perhaps, but did you ever *ask* Jenny that?"

Dan paused, letting the little voice that had been niggling in the back of his mind all weekend be heard. "We were dating. Naturally, I assumed the child was mine."

"But you never specifically asked, did you?"

Guilt and embarrassment burned at the base of his spine, and he banged the stack of charts on his desk. "Is there a purpose to your visit, Mr. Warren, or are you here to mock me for being duped by her?"

"Please, call me Mike. And yes, there is a purpose to my visit." He sat as quietly as a mediating monk, the only perceptible movement being the slight twitching of his lips.

Dan slumped back in his desk chair and swiveled around. "I'm listening."

"First, let me clarify my relationship to Jenny. I'm married to her brother, Jason."

Dan stiffened, then leaned forward. "You're gay?"

Mike nodded. "Do you find that surprising?"

"Sorry, I just assumed..." Sweat beaded along the back of his neck. This conversation had just made an awkward turn. "But if you're married to her brother, then why are you sleeping with her?"

"Dr. Kelly, as a medical professional, surely you've heard of something called artificial insemination."

"So you didn't sleep with her?"

Mike shook his head.

Oh, shit!

A new line of moisture formed along his hairline, and the mounting pressure of his pounding heart mimicked his response to a stressful case in the operating room where one small move could spell disaster. He couldn't have been more wrong about Jenny, and now he was on the hot seat, getting grilled by her lawyer brother-in-law.

"No matter how many advances reproductive medicine has made, two men can't create a baby. We still need a woman for that. Jenny agreed to act as surrogate for us since her DNA is closest to her brother's. She underwent artificial insemination the week before Comic-Con and was already pregnant when she met you, even though we didn't have confirmation of it until she returned home."

Suddenly everything started to make sense. Why she'd pushed him away from the beginning. Why she said she couldn't get involved with anyone. Why she wouldn't give any reason other than it was complicated.

Complicated didn't begin to describe this.

"So you're fairly certain the baby's yours?" he asked.

"She had a positive test the Sunday after Comic-Con. How early do you think a home test can detect a pregnancy?"

"Ten days after conception at the earliest." Which only confirmed that the baby wasn't his. The familiar ache returned to his chest. He still wanted the child.

He still wanted her.

"Jenny claims she told you that she was pregnant and that you seemed fine with it at the time."

He searched his memory until he zeroed on something she'd whispered as he was falling asleep the night he'd confronted her about the pregnancy. Something about being pregnant when she'd met him. But he'd always assumed she was referring to when she ran into him again at Paul's game. And he'd been so scared that she'd push him away that he didn't dare ask too many questions.

"I can understand that you were upset to learn the baby wasn't yours, Dr. Kelly, but I thought I would let you know the circumstances surrounding Jenny's pregnancy. She's giving us the one thing we can't have, and I'm sorry to hear her generosity has caused conflict in your relationship."

Translation: I'm a complete asshole for dumping her.

"Jenny had mentioned that up until this weekend, you'd insisted on coming to her ultrasound tomorrow where we find out the baby's gender. I hope you'll reconsider and join us." Mike stood and smoothed his tie. "Have a good day, Dr. Kelly."

Dan stared straight ahead, his fist pressed against his mouth, long after Mike had left. He'd been so convinced that Jenny had cheated on him that he didn't bother to look for another explanation. And now that he had it...

I'm a dick of the first degree.

He picked up his phone and checked his missed calls. After leaving her condo Friday night, he'd blocked her number. A quick scan showed she'd called him twenty-three times since then, but she'd only left one voicemail. His hand shook as he typed in his PIN and listened to it.

Her voice was quiet and raw, and she sniffled once while speaking. *Shit!* He'd made her cry. It wasn't a long explanation or a series of excuses. Just a simple plea to let her explain. But it was the last three words of her message that ripped him apart.

She loved him.

Neither one of them had mentioned the L-word while they were together, even though he'd been tempted to say it more than once. Now Jenny had beaten him to it. Even after he'd run out on her, she still loved him.

He replayed the voicemail once more time, his breath

catching as he listened to her say "I love you" again. He could get used to that phrase, but only if it came from her. He hung up and found her number. He should call her back, let her know he was sorry and that he knew everything. But somehow, saying he was sorry didn't seem like enough. He needed to do something more than just tell her. He needed to show her.

He switched to Adam's number and waited for his brother to pick up. "I need a crash course on Groveling 101."

"And you think I have any experience in that department?" his brother shot back.

"Well, it was either you or Frank, but since you're married…"

Adam chuckled. "So you heard Jenny's side of the story?"

"Yeah, and it's a doozy. One that's going to require more than a bouquet of flowers to smooth over."

"You have my full attention."

He recounted Mike's visit to Adam, and by the time he hung up, he had a game plan to win her back.

***

Jenny sat on the ultrasound table and cast a worried glance to her brother and Mike. Dan hadn't shown up. She'd purposely scheduled the ultrasound for this time because it was between surgeries on his OR day.

"Maybe the case ran over," Jason suggested.

She shook her head and hoisted her legs up. "He's not coming."

"I'm sorry, Jenny," Mike said, holding her brother's hand and reminding her of how a loving couple should be.

"I thought I'd gotten through to him yesterday."

"I underestimated how proud he could be." She reclined against the pillows and lifted her tunic to expose her bump as the technician came in. "But please, don't worry about me. This day is for you two. Let's find out what you're having."

She tried to keep her voice cheerful, even though she was on the verge of bawling. She had a love–hate relationship with this baby. Even though it was the reason why Dan had left her—just like she'd known he would from the beginning—she still was reluctant to let go of it. It was Mike and Jason's child, but it was still hers, too. And every kick reminded her that she would have to give it up to them once it was born.

Only after today, it wouldn't be an "it." They'd know the baby's gender, making it all the more real. Soon, she'd start referring to the baby as he or she. Mike and Jason might even decide on a name today, and she would become even more attached to it. Bitterness rose into her throat. This should be her baby, not theirs. She possessively braced her hands on the sides of her belly and wondered why she'd agreed to do this in the first place.

But once she saw excitement on their faces, her anger faded. She could let go—for them.

"Hi, I'm Susie," the tech said in a cheerful voice. "You must be Jenny." She squirted the warm gel over Jenny's stomach. "And which one of you is the father?"

"We both are," Mike said, looking down adoringly at his husband.

Susie's eyes widened, and her mouth bobbed while she tried to find something to say.

For the past five months, Jenny had dreaded this type of reaction, but now that she'd come face to face with it, it was easy to say, "I'm the auntie surrogate."

The tech's brows drew together for a few seconds before it dawned on her. "Oh, I see. Well, then, let's see how this baby's doing. You can see what I see on the TV over there."

Jason and Mike stood in front of it, their attention fully focused on the blank sixty-inch screen. Their excitement helped dull her pain. At least she wouldn't be able to see anything with them blocking her view.

Just as Susie placed the transducer to Jenny's stomach, the door opened, and Dan's shadow stretched across the darkened room. "Am I too late?" he asked.

Her pulse quickened, but she couldn't force her tongue to work. He was here.

And if he was, did that mean he forgave her?

"Just in time," Mike answered.

"Good." Dan gave the men a curt nod of acknowledgment and then sat down in the chair beside the bed. He was still dressed in scrubs with a blue surgical cap covering his hair like he'd just run over from the operating room. He took her hand in his and placed a kiss in her palm, his gaze never leaving her face. "Today was more complicated than I'd first thought. I'm sorry."

Even though he appeared to be apologizing for the ultrasound, his expression said more. The plea in his eyes, the softness of his mouth, the tender way he cradled her hand in his. He was apologizing for everything that had happened over the last few days.

Unshed tears stung her eyes. Relief flooded her,

followed by a sense of peace. Having Dan by her side would make today and the rest of the pregnancy easier to bear. She might not be able to keep the baby, but she had him. "If anyone should be apologizing, it's me."

"Shh." He brushed a strand of hair out of her face and tilted his head toward her brother and Mike. "We can talk about this later. Let's not hold things up any longer."

A series of images flashed on the screen as Susie ran the transducer over Jenny's stomach. Shadows moved and swayed in a confusing jumble of white and gray. Then Susie stilled and twisted the transducer.

A profile came into focus.

"Oh my God, look at his little nose," Jason said, pointing to the screen.

Jenny's throat tightened as she looked on her baby's face. For weeks, she'd barely believed there was another person inside her, but once she saw the face, it became real.

A glance out of the corner of her eye told her Dan felt the same way. He stared at the screen, his Adam's apple bobbing up and down, his face drawn with an unreadable emotion. She squeezed his hand, and he turned away and gave her a weak smile. He didn't have to say what he was feeling. She saw the flicker of grief in his eyes. For weeks, he'd thought this baby was his, and he was still coming to terms with the loss.

Susie typed with one hand and clicked her mouse. The printer at the bottom of the stand sputtered to life and spat out a long sheet of paper. "Okay, we have some baby pictures here. Now, do we want to know the sex?"

"Absolutely," Jason answered. "We have a meeting

with the interior decorator tomorrow to finalize the color scheme of the nursery."

Dan's lips twitched in amusement, and he placed another kiss on her hand. He was probably relieved he wouldn't have to find a bigger place and prepare a room for the baby like he'd talked about on Friday.

Susie moved the transducer further down, pausing a second to purse her lips and frown before continuing on. "Here are the legs. Let's see if baby wants to cooperate with us."

She rotated the device around and clicked a button, freezing the image. Then she drew an arrow to the cleft and typed, "It's a girl!"

Mike sank into the nearest chair, his dark skin ashen. He ran his hand over his face in an uncharacteristic show of fear. "A girl?"

"I'll be fine, Mike." Jason gave his husband a reassuring hug. "Think about this way—we don't have to explain liking girls to her."

"Unless she's gay," Mike replied with a half laugh. He puffed out his cheeks and blew the air out. "Oh, mama. We're having a girl."

"Speaking of mamas, we should probably call ours and give the good news." Jason pulled Mike back up to his feet. "Let's go out to the waiting room so we don't distract Susie from her work."

"I'll take some more pics along the way, but you've already seen the exciting stuff," she said before turning off the TV and focusing on her monitor. Her smile seemed forced as they left, and it faded once she moved the ultrasound to the spot she'd paused at before.

154

A trickle of fear wormed up Jenny's spine. Something was wrong.

Dan let go of her hand and rose from the chair, moving behind Susie. He stared at the screen, his hand covering his mouth while she snapped more images and typed a few words here and there.

The minutes ticked by in silence, each one multiplying the dread swirling inside Jenny's stomach. How could the baby who had seemed so alive and perfect moments before have something wrong with it? Dozens of scenarios entered her mind, each one worse than the one before it. Finally, she found the courage to ask, "What is it?"

Both Dan and Susie snapped their heads to her, then at each other. An unspoken conversation passed between them that ended when Jason and Mike came back into the room.

"Did we miss anything?" Mike asked, clearly over his initial shock on learning he was having a daughter.

"Dan?" she asked.

The atmosphere in the room chilled, and Dan backed away from the ultrasound machine. "I'm not an OB or a radiologist."

"But you see something, don't you?" Jenny propped herself up on her elbows. "There's something wrong with the baby."

"I didn't say that." He took a few more steps toward the door and turned to Mike and Jason. "It's not my area of expertise."

Impatience lit with the fear brewing her chest and exploded. "Tell me, Dan."

He looked one more time at the two lawyers in the

room and shook his head. "I can't."

Mike nodded solemnly and placed his hand on Jason's shoulder. "What he means is that from a medical–legal standpoint, it's something beyond his training where he could be held accountable if he's wrong."

Dan pressed his lips together as though he wanted to tell him what he saw but was forcing himself not to speak. He looked down at the ground and took another step back.

"Damn it, Dan, I don't care!" She sat up and jumped off the bed, pushing Susie out of her way. "Tell me."

A stony stare was all she got in response.

His pager went off, and he lifted it to read the number. "My next case is ready. I need to go back to the OR."

Her breath came sharp and fast, and the room spun around her. Jason and Mike flanked her and led her back to the bed before her knees gave out. A hot tear streaked down her cheek, and Dan winced.

"I'm sorry, Jenny. We'll talk later tonight."

He disappeared before she could say anything else. The earlier joy of having him back vanished, leaving an uncertain emptiness that would plague her until she knew the truth about her child.

Chapter Fourteen

Dan massaged the back of his neck and sat in his car. It had been one hell of a day so far, but it wasn't over yet. He stared up at Jenny's condo, trying to figure out how to break the news to her gently. He'd told the truth when he'd said that he wasn't trained to read a fetal ultrasound, but he'd seen enough in his career to know what he was looking at. One glance at the screen told him what was wrong with the baby.

Intestines did not belong outside the abdominal cavity.

The light coming from her window told him she was still up, maybe waiting for him. He'd wrapped up his last case hours ago. The rest of the afternoon had been spent in the hospital's NICU, talking to the perinatologist and gathering information for Jenny, Jason, and Mike. If he was going to deliver bad news, hopefully, he could soften the blow by letting them know what to expect. He was armed with informational booklets, names of OBs specializing in high-risk cases and pediatric surgeons, numbers for Seattle Children's Hospital, and web addresses for online support groups. But more important, he was committed to staying by Jenny's side throughout all of this like he would if it were his own kid.

He rubbed his chest. The ache there still lingered. The ultrasound had revived the intensity of it like reopening a half-healed wound. He'd seen the baby's face on the screen and wished with all his heart that it had been his child's. Even after he'd seen the bowel floating around in the amniotic fluid, he still wanted the child. It wasn't until he was on his way over here that he realized why.

It was because the child was Jenny's.

And even though he wasn't going to be a father, he could still be the man she leaned on when she needed strength. He could give her that much.

And maybe so much more if she would take him back.

He gathered up the stack of papers and pamphlets and climbed the stairs to her condo, his heart thudding with each heavy step. As a surgeon, he'd given bad news more times than he'd wanted to, but this time, it was to someone he loved.

Jenny was sitting on the couch between Jason and Mike, staring blankly ahead with a nearly empty tissue box nestled between her legs. Her eyes were red-rimmed and raw, her cheeks blotchy. She sniffled once before turning those mournful dark eyes on him.

Her grief hit him like a punch in the gut. God, he wanted to do nothing more than gather her up in his arms and hold her until he convinced her that everything would be all right. But the two men on either side of her kept him from doing that. As long as he was under the watchful eyes of men who were both her brothers and lawyers, he had to retain some semblance of professionalism.

"My OB called this afternoon asking me to come into

tomorrow to discuss the ultrasound," Jenny said, her voice hollow. "She wouldn't tell me why, either."

Dan pulled out a chair from the small dining table and turned it around so he could straddle it. The high wooden back offered him some restraint as he replied, "Now that we're alone, I can tell you what I saw, if you want to know."

Jenny looked at her brother, then at Mike before nodding. "We all want to know, and even if you're wrong, we'd still appreciate your opinion and will not hold you accountable."

He wanted to laugh at her carefully schooled response. Mike must have coached her while they were waiting. "Good to know I'm not in danger of being held liable." He laid the stack of papers on the table and took a deep breath. "The baby has gastroschisis."

Jenny's brows angled down in confusion. "What?"

"Gastroschisis. It's where there's a defect in the abdominal wall that allows parts of the intestine to escape." He handed the pamphlet explaining the condition to her. "That's what I saw in the ultrasound."

Mike and Jason huddled around her to read over her shoulders. "And you're fairly certain that's what you saw?" Mike asked.

"I'd say about ninety-five percent certain. I know bowel when I see it."

Mike narrowed his eyes, ready to pick apart his assessment. "And the other five percent?"

"The slight chance that this could be a loose omphalocele or perhaps a very odd-looking umbilical cord. But what goes against either is that an omphalocele has a membrane around it that keeps the intestines contained, and the umbilical cord has a distinctive blood flow appearance on ultrasound."

"So you're fairly certain?" Jenny repeated.

Dan hugged the chair back and nodded. He was almost a hundred percent certain, but his years of medical training had taught him that nothing was ever one hundred percent. He'd seen patients survive the odds just like he'd seen routine conditions turn lethal. The human body still amazed and surprised him with its fortitude and fragility.

"So what does this mean for our daughter?" Jason asked.

"It means she probably won't come home with you until she's about a month old, give or take a few weeks." He handed them the list of providers. "Your OB will probably refer you to a high-risk OB for continued monitoring. You should be able to deliver her normally, and once she's born, one of the perinatologists will assess her and take her to Children's. From there, the surgeons will help return the bowel to the abdomen and stitch it closed."

Jenny looked up from the paperwork. "And that will take a month?"

Dan shook his head. "No, that's the easy part. The hard part will be getting her bowels to start working properly so she can eat and grow. That's what takes the longest time, according to the perinatologist I spoke to this afternoon."

Jenny distributed some of the information to her brother and brother-in-law. After they swapped it around and read, Mike asked, "What's the survival rate?"

"Almost a hundred percent. Most of the kids do well and only have a tiny scar to show for it. They grow up to live normal lives."

Jenny's lower lip quivered, and she lowered her eyes. "And what are the chances this will happen again?"

"Very low. As far as we know, it's not genetic, and there's no known cause. It's just one of those freak things that happen."

Her shoulders dropped, and she closed her eyes. Relief washed over her features. "Thank you, Dan."

"Yes, thank you," Jason echoed. "You're been more than helpful. Mike and I are going to take all of this home and read through it." He didn't have to add that he was leaving his sister in Dan's care.

The married couple rose, and each one gave Jenny a kiss on the cheek. Mike held out his hand to Dan. "I appreciate you putting all this together for us and answering our questions. Is there any chance you could perform the surgery she needs?"

"I appreciate the sentiment, but I'm going to leave this to the experts." He stood and shook Mike's hand, and then Jason's. "Apparently, the guys at Children's see at least twenty of these a year, so they know exactly what needs to be done to get her home to you as quickly as possible."

"Good to know." Jason waved to Jenny before following his husband out of the condo.

Jenny stayed where she was, tearing her damp tissue into tiny little pieces. "So I didn't do anything wrong to hurt the baby?"

"Absolutely not." He sat next her and put his arm

around her shoulder.

"I was so scared that I had. From the moment I saw the look on the ultrasound tech's face, I knew something was wrong, and all I could think about was how I'd messed up Mike and Jason's child."

He tilted her chin up to face him. "It's your child, too, Jenny."

"I know. That's what makes this all so hard." She grabbed a fresh tissue and dabbed her eyes before burying her face in the space between his neck and shoulder. "I tried so hard not to get attached to her because I knew the minute she was born, she'd be taken away from me, but it's hard not to love a child when you feel her kick you every day or see her face on the screen or know she's going to need surgery as soon as she's born."

The ache flared again in his chest, and he squeezed his arms around her. "I know."

"Shit, Dan, I'm sorry." She lifted her head. "I guess if there's a silver lining to all this, it's that it isn't your child who has her intestines protruding from her stomach."

"Nothing's changed the way I feel about her." He rested his hand on her belly, wishing he could feel the baby moving inside like she did. "Even though I know she isn't my child, she's still a part of you, and that's reason enough for me to love her."

Her breath caught, and her lips parted. "You love her, even though she's not yours?"

He ran his fingers along her tear-streaked cheek, rubbing away some of the fine grains of salt that clung to her skin. Why was it so easy to tell her he loved a person he'd never seen, never held in his arms, and yet so frightening to tell her the exact same words? "At first I was disappointed. I was really looking forward to becoming a father, to raising a family of my own. And when I learned the baby wasn't mine, well, I…"

Shame rolled through his gut like a poorly cooked meal, and he turned away. "I've been a selfish asshole, Jenny. I was so upset to learn the baby wasn't mine that I forgot the most important thing in all this. You were mine. You have such a generous heart to do something like this for your brother, but all I could see was you had something that didn't belong to me. I forgot to see that you were willing to open your heart up to me, even though I'd done nothing to deserve a place there."

She silenced him by placing her finger on his lips. The dull sorrow that had filled her eyes since he'd arrived broke away like clouds after the rain, revealing the warm light shining behind them. Her smile was as bright as the sun. It chased away the last shadows of doubt that had plagued him. "I love you, too, Dan."

He lowered her hand and said, "I know, because you said it first. But if you let me, I'll spend the rest of my days telling you how much I love you."

"Don't tell me. Show me." She pulled him closer and kissed him.

He tried to ignore the desire she sparked within him from the moment their lips touched, but it was so entwined with the love he felt for her that it was impossible to separate the two emotions. He let them dance through his veins to the slow, sensual tempo she set with her tongue. The salt from her tears mingled with the sweetness of her mouth. He pulled her closer, his arousal increasing with every decadent kiss until he was on the verge of making love to her right there. Based on the way she clung to him, she wouldn't stop him. But he needed to stop.

He wasn't nearly done apologizing to her.

He pulled away, his breath shaking, and said, "There's more. I want you to have this."

Her mouth formed a perfect circle, and her panic flashed in her eyes as he reached into his pocket. "Dan, I—"

She fell silent when he pressed the red, twenty-sided piece of plastic into her hand. Wonder and surprise lit up her face as she rolled it across her palm. "Your lucky die?"

"I don't need it anymore. I figure as long as I have you, I'm the luckiest man in the world."

Jenny threw her arms around his neck and hugged him. "Thank you, Dan."

Then she pulled away, her face more serious. "I admit, I was a bit worried it was something else."

"A ring?" he teased. Not that he hadn't thought of it. But somehow, proposing to her didn't seem like the best idea after delivering the bad news.

Color filled her cheeks, and she looked away. "Is it silly of me to think such a thing?"

"Not at all." He brushed his hand through her silky black hair. "If I offered one to you, would you take it?"

She hesitated for a moment, puffing her cheeks out as she held her breath. "Maybe."

"Maybe?" He repeated her response, his pride bearing the brunt of her blow.

"I think we need to start over, Dan. Be honest from

the beginning, and not keep secrets from each other. Or, at least, I do." She removed his hands and pressed them into his lap, her voice as serious as the announcer who lists all the warnings at the end of a pharmaceutical commercial. "Hi, I'm Hue Jenny Nguyen. I'm a total geek who designs robots for a living. My mother is the poster child for insane tiger moms, but my dad is kind of cool. My brother is gay and married to a black man. And, oh, by the way, I'm carrying their child."

"Trying to scare me away?"

Her lips twitched, and she shook her head. "Just want to make sure you know what you're getting yourself into if you want to date me."

"Fine, but now it's my turn. Hi, I'm Daniel Kelly. I'm a geek, too, who uses robots to perform surgeries for a living. My mom seems patient, but she's always hinting that she wants grandchildren. I have six brothers, some of whom are celebrities, making me probably the most boring in the bunch." He lowered his voice and leaned closer. "And I happen to find pregnant women very attractive."

She laughed, the sound clear and light after all the gloom and darkness of the day. "So you find big bellies and cankles sexy?"

"Um-hmm." He caressed her bump and pressed his lips to the nape of her neck. "I'd be lying if I said I didn't like your new curves." He cupped one of her breasts and kissed the top of the rounded mound. "Especially these curves."

"Keep talking like that, and you'll get me naked on the first date."

"I already did that." Memories of their first night together flashed though his mind, and his dick responded like an overeager teenage boy's. As much as he wanted to draw that pebbled nipple into his mouth, he forced his lips up her neck toward her jaw. "I want more than just you naked in my bed. I want to make you come. I want to make you feel worshipped and adored. I want you to know that I find every delicious inch of you sexy."

She dug her fingers into his thighs and arched her neck back. "I find that hard to believe while we're both still wearing our clothes."

"Are you calling me a liar?"

"Let's see what the die says. High, he's telling the truth. Low, he's just trying to get into my panties."

"I'm trying to get into your panties, regardless," he said with a growl of need.

She rolled the die on the coffee table.

Fourteen.

"Maybe the die isn't quite in tune with me yet. Let me roll it again."

He grabbed her hand before she could retrieve the die, lifted her up in his arms, and carried her into the bedroom. "It's just a stupid piece of plastic anyway."

"Not to me." She turned his face to hers and kissed him long after he'd laid her on the bed.

Chapter Fifteen

The baby kicked harder than usual as though she sensed her mother's anxiety. Jenny rested her hand on the growing bump that now took over her entire lap and willed the baby to be still. Her stomach was already tied in enough knots to make a *kinbaku* master proud. Tonight was the night she was taking Dan to formally meet her parents.

Unlike most girls, it wasn't her father she worried about. It was her mom. Her father would likely greet Dan in his calm manner, ask a few questions, and nod pleasantly since he knew how much Jenny already loved him. Her mother, on the other hand, would likely interrogate Dan with a slew of inappropriate questions about topics ranging from his income to his zodiac sign. Jenny had put off this meeting as long as she could, but when her parents specially invited Dan over to their house to celebrate Chinese New Year, she knew her time was up.

At least it will be a small family gathering, she said to herself as Dan exited off Ruston Way toward her parents' house. *Nothing too extreme.*

She should've known better than to expect that.

"Is there some kind of block party happening tonight?" Dan asked, peering down the crowded street.

The rapid-fire explosion of firecrackers answered him.

Shit!

The closer they got to her parents' place, the more congested the street became. Every light was on in the house—something her skinflint mother normally didn't allow—and red lanterns hung from the eaves. Shadows moved in front of the windows, and Vietnamese music blared into the neighborhood when a group of kids with sparklers ran out the front door to set off another brick of firecrackers.

Jenny closed her eyes and massaged her temples. "Welcome to Chinese New Year."

Dan chuckled and drove past her parents' home. They ended up having to go the next block over to find a parking spot. The cold February air whipped around her ankles when she got out, and an icy mist formed in front of her mouth with every breath she exhaled. The weather forecast called for possible snow tomorrow, but tonight, the air was crisp and dry. A red firework bloomed in the starry sky overhead, followed a chorus of shouts from the excited children gathered in her parents' front yard.

However, as soon as she and Dan entered the yard, the children swarmed around them and threatened to knock the potted orchids from her arms. *"Chúc Mừng Năm Mới,"* they cried over and over again.

Embarrassment flamed her cheeks as she heard the Tết greeting. Traditionally, elders gave envelopes with money to children as part of the New Year celebrations, but her mother hadn't told her that there would be guests over tonight.

She opened her mouth to apologize, but stopped when Dan pulled a stack of red envelopes out of his coat pocket.

"Happy New Year," he said as he gave each child his or her gift.

"How did you know?" she whispered, grateful he'd spared her the shame of showing up empty handed.

Dan grinned as the last child ran off. "Jason called me this morning and gave me a heads up."

"I didn't know he had your number." Over the past couple of months, they'd met up with Jason and Mike for dinner, but she'd never suspected they interacted without her.

"Of course he does. I've even played basketball a few times with him and Mike."

"Hiding any more secrets from me?"

"Maybe." He opened the door, ignoring the blast of music that greeted them, and waited for her to enter.

The house was packed with her parents' friends and family, all chatting with each other in Vietnamese. Dozens of voices tried to talk over each other, but the moment Dan closed the door, they all grew silent and turned toward them.

Dan ran his finger along his collar and wore a forced smile.

Jenny tried not to laugh. It must've been hard for him to be the only white person with a crowd of Vietnamese looking up at him.

Jason made his way through the crowd and gave her a hug. "*Chúc Mừng Năm Mới*, little sis."

"*An khang thịnh vượng,*" she replied, wishing her brother security, good health, and prosperity.

"It's already going to be a good year." He laid his hand on her stomach, receiving a kick from the baby, before moving on to shake Dan's hand. "Happy New Year."

"The same to you." His voice sounded tense, strained, as though he was nervous. Normally, he and Jason got along with ease.

Gooseflesh prickled her arms. Something was up, and she suspected the two men had plotted a way to win over her mother.

"Come on in and meet our parents," Jason said, leading them toward the great room where the family altar was set up.

Her parents stood proudly in front of the table covered with offerings to the ancestors and household gods. Chrysanthemums and peach blossoms flanked the sides, and a large tray with mangos, coconuts, and other fruits sat in the center. Red scrolls adorned with black and gold calligraphy adorned the walls, proclaiming "Happy Spring" and "A Prosperous New Year." Everything seemed normal for Tết.

Too normal, considering the circumstances.

Jenny forced a smile on her face. "Mom, Dad, this is my boyfriend, Dan. Dan, this is my father, Binh, and my mother, Phuong."

Dan, for his part, seemed to have been well schooled by Jason. He bowed his head politely to her mother, who remained silent, and extended his hand to her father.

"It is a pleasure to finally meet you," her father said in his quiet, balanced way. "I have heard many good things about you from my son and daughter."

Her mother remained silent, a sure sign that she was not particularly happy with her daughter bringing a non-Vietnamese man home for such an important occasion. She visually dissected her guest, and the tense lines around her mouth reminded Jenny about their last meeting, when Dan came out of her bedroom half naked.

Jenny's hands started to tremble. She held up the orchids. "I've brought a gift to honor our ancestors."

Some of the disapproval faded from her mother's eyes. "You may place it at the altar."

They stepped aside to let her approach the table. She placed the pot on the table and knelt before it, praying to her ancestors that her parents would learn to love Dan as much as she did.

***

Dan stood behind Jenny as she sat on the floor with some of the children and tossed the three dice. She'd explained that *Bầu cua cá cọp* was a traditional game played on Chinese New Year, and after watching it for a while, he realized it was a simple version of craps. Each die had an animal on the side that corresponded to the animals on the board. The players would all place bets on what animals they thought would show up on the next roll. The more times the animal showed up, the more they won.

Jenny was the only adult playing, but it didn't seem to matter to her. She seemed far more at ease with the children than the other adults. Her laughter was infectious, and her smile lit up the room. He wanted to wrap her up in his arms and kiss her every time she looked up at him, but he'd been warned by Jason that public displays of affection between members of the opposite sex were considered taboo.

He reached into his pocket instead, no longer missing his lucky die since giving it to her months ago. Tonight, however, his fingers wrapped around the small velvet box he'd brought with him. Jason had explained that Vietnamese engagements were complicated affairs, but he could start by asking her parents tonight to see if they would be agreeable to letting him marry Jenny.

It was near midnight when her father approached him and said quietly, "Please, Dan, I would be honored if you would step outside with me for a few minutes."

It was the first time one of her parents had spoken to him since they'd arrived. Jenny was far too wrapped up in the game to notice, so he nodded and followed Binh outside to the backyard.

A chilly fog had rolled in from the sound and blanketed the outside world in misty silence. They moved to where the glow of the lights from the windows and sounds of the party inside faded. Dan's heart pounded. This was his chance to ask for Jenny's hand, but his mouth seemed too dry to form coherent words.

"My son mentioned you wished to speak to me about my daughter," Binh started.

"I do, but I have no idea where to start. I wish to respect your customs, but I also know I am a stranger to them."

Binh nodded, and the corners of his mouth twitched. "We both know my daughter does not adhere to traditional customs very well, so speak from yours."

He reached into his pocket and squeezed the ring box. "I'd like to marry her."

"Even though she is pregnant with another man's child?"

He nodded. "If anything, it makes me love her all the more for what she offered to do."

"So you love her?"

His tongue loosened. "Very much so."

"And you will provide for her and do all that you can to keep her safe and happy?"

"I would."

"Then I do not object to your match." Binh nodded to the party inside. "But now comes the difficult part. Convincing her mother you are a worthy match."

"Would this be the part where saying I'm a doctor helps?"

Binh chuckled and checked his watch. "Perhaps, but I have a better idea. Let's go back inside."

The clock was striking midnight as they opened the door. Binh stood back and let Dan enter first. The crowd stilled as all turned in his direction.

For the second time that evening, Dan's collar choked him. He'd always hated being the center of attention.

Jenny's mother made her way through the crowd and bowed her head. "We welcome you into our home as the first visitor of the new year."

A murmur swept through their guests, but unfortunately, he didn't understand a word of it.

Jason appeared at his side. "Well played."

Dan turned to him and whispered, "I don't understand."

"You're the *xông đất*. According to tradition, the first guest a family receives after Tết determines the family's fortune for the entire year. With you being a successful doctor who's obviously smitten with my fruitful sister, it's a very good thing."

Phuong waved him into the living room with an open palm. "Please come in and have some *Mứt.*"

He turned to Jason for guidance. "Is this a good thing, too?"

"Any time my mother isn't shrieking at you is a good sign." Jason patted him on the back and pushed him forward. "She's offering you food."

He came into the living room to find Jenny standing beside her father, her dark eyes dancing with amusement as she offered him a bowl with candied fruits in it. "Try them. It's the only time of the year they're served."

He took a handful and chewed on the sweetened dried mangos while he looked to Binh for a clue to when he could pop the question.

Her father nodded and turned to address his guests. "We are honored to have Dr. Daniel Kelly as our guest tonight for many reasons, the foremost being that he has requested my daughter's hand in marriage."

Jenny drew in a sharp breath. Her hand fell to her stomach. "You did?"

"I even bought you a ring." He began to pull it out of his pocket when Phuong rushed between them to stop him.

"No, this is not the way it's done." She turned to him. "If you wish to marry my daughter, then we will do it the

174

Vietnamese way."

Confusion swirled with desperation inside his chest. He'd done the proper thing and asked her father. All he wanted to do now was give Jenny her ring, take her home, and start planning the rest of their lives together. But Phuong had to step in and steal his moment.

Jenny's brow creased. "Mom, that's not necessary for me."

"It is for our family. I will consult with the fortune-teller to find a date for the engagement ceremony." She turned and made her way through the crowd to a gray-haired woman.

"I knew Mom wouldn't make this easy," Jenny muttered under her breath.

His palms itched to touch her, to hold her close and kiss her in front of everyone. "But you are worth it."

The worry vanished from her face, and she moved closer to him. "And you assumed I'd say yes," she teased.

And just like that, he knew she would. His rattled nerves eased. She was everything he'd dreamed of and more, a Buttercup to his Westley. Whatever she asked of him, he'd reply, "As you wish."

He took her hand in his, defying what was consider proper behavior. "You can always say no. I've been holding on to the ring for a few weeks already, just waiting for a chance to ask your father's permission."

"He's not the one you have to win over." She nodded toward her mother, who was in the midst of a furious discussion in Vietnamese with the fortune-teller.

"They say Vegas is really nice this time of year," he murmured. "We could always elope."

"It's tempting. Too bad they closed the *Star Trek* exhibit there. We could've gotten married on the deck of the *Enterprise*."

He grinned. If there was ever a doubt how well they fit together, she erased it by suggesting a wedding venue fit for a true geek.

Phuong nodded a few more times before returning to them. "It would be a very lucky day for you two if we had the engagement ceremony in two weeks and two days."

"Think you can get your mom and brothers out here that quickly?" Jenny's voice rose with a hint of panic.

"Of course," he replied, even though he was still baffled why he'd need them. "Unless you'd like to wait until after the baby's born."

"No," Phuong declared. "It would be unlucky to wait. Two weeks and two days will be very lucky."

"You wanted to be part of this insanity." Jenny raised one brow. "I would've been happy with sneaking off to Vegas."

"Too late now." He bowed to her parents. "I will arrange to have my family here on that day for the engagement ceremony."

"Then let us move forward with the planning." Binh took Jenny's hand and placed it in Dan's. "I would like to welcome you to our family."

The guests lined up to offer their congratulations, sometimes in English, sometimes in Vietnamese where Jenny would translate for them. An hour later, he was ready to leave when Jenny suggested it. His face ached from smiling, and he couldn't wait to get her alone. But on the way out, he finally caught an approving smile from

Phuong.

Mission accomplished.

When they got to his car, he pulled Jenny to him and kissed her like he'd been wanting to do all night. "I can't wait to get you home and celebrate tonight properly."

"There's only one problem." She pressed her palm against his chest and pushed him away. "You still haven't officially asked me if I want to marry you."

He waved his arm out into the swirling fog. "Now?"

She lifted her chin and nodded.

"Here?"

"The sooner you do it, the sooner we can properly celebrate."

Dan got down on one knee, ignoring the icy chill that bled through his dress slacks, and pulled out the ring he'd been waiting to give her. "Jenny, would you marry me?"

Tears formed along the crinkles of her eyes. "Yes, I'll marry you."

He stood and kissed her again, this time receiving what he hoped was a swift kick of approval from the baby. When he finally pulled away, he opened the car door for her. "So explain this Vietnamese engagement ceremony to me."

"It starts with you being sucker enough to agree to it."

He winced. "That bad?"

"Let's just say you're going to owe your brothers big time."

Chapter Sixteen

The dress was too tight.

Jenny gritted her teeth and tried to calm her breathing, but no matter what she did, the red *áo dài* squeezed around her stomach like a corset. The sensation came in rhythmic waves before loosening up again. She'd just about convinced herself it was all due to nerves when the next wave would hit.

Dì Tam waltzed into the bedroom and gave her a once-over. "You look pretty enough to be a bride."

"Too bad I feel like a whale in this thing." She tugged on the dress again, wondering what her aunt would do if she *accidentally* ripped the silk fabric that strained over her bump.

"That is what you get for being pregnant with another man's child. You are very lucky that a doctor wants to marry you."

She rolled her eyes and waddled over to the chair her aunt held out for her. The ceremony would be starting in less than thirty minutes, and she still needed to do her hair and makeup for the pictures. While her aunt fussed over her hair and arranged the traditional combs, she rubbed her stomach. The baby had been unusually still today, and worry gnawed at her gut.

Her mother joined them and cast one glance at Jenny's feet. "You painted your nails."

Like I could reach my toes in my condition. Luckily, Maureen had arrived yesterday and treated her to a pre-engagement ceremony spa day. The relaxing massage and pedicure soothed her jitters and made today more bearable.

"Did his family arrive?" her mother asked before grabbing the eyeliner.

"Yes, they did." Last night, she and Dan had dinner with his family in a private room of a local restaurant. Five of his brothers had made it. Ben had to miss the ceremony due to a game, but Hailey had come down, proudly displaying her own bump to the family. The meal was full of teasing and laughter, but by the time it ended, she felt like she was already part of the Kelly family.

It would be a very different scene today when the boisterous and laid-back Kellys met the straight-laced Vietnamese traditions of the Nguyen family. She only hoped that once the formalities were over, the reception would be just as fun as last night's dinner had been.

Her stomach tightened again, forcing the air from her lungs. The baby wasn't due for another month, but according to the birthing class instructor, the contractions could start at any time now.

Her mother paused and sent her a worried look. "Do you need some water?"

She shook her head. What she wouldn't give to be wearing the loose-fitting dress she wore last night. "The baby's just misbehaving."

"The baby is your child." Her mother went back to applying her makeup.

No, the baby is Mike and Jason's, not mine.

Jenny closed her eyes and focused on taking deep breaths. Her ultrasound two days ago looked reassuring, according to her OB. With the exception of the exposed bowel, the baby was doing fine. This was all due to nerves.

Jason popped his head in. "The guests are starting to arrive."

Her mother added one swipe of lip gloss. "Only family inside. The rest will have to wait until the groom's family enters."

"Ten-four, *Má*." Jason gave them a playful salute and went back into the living room to divert traffic.

Anxiety formed at the base of Jenny's spine, stretching around her belly and squeezing. For the hundredth time today, she wished Dan hadn't agreed to this ceremony. Yes, it was a peace offering to get on her mother's good side, but she would be dreading it until it was over.

At least she'd gotten her parents to agree to let them have a quiet marriage ceremony after the baby was born.

"Stand up," Dì Tam ordered. She stood next to Phuong and visually picked Jenny apart. "It is too bad you are pregnant."

"Dan and I were willing to wait until after the baby was born."

Her mother shook her head. "No, today is a lucky day."

Jason reappeared. "Dan and his family just drove up."

She sent him a worried look, hoping Dan and his brothers remembered all the intricacies involved from the red cloth-covered boxes containing traditional gifts to the proper order of entering the household. "Maybe I should go out there and explain things one more time."

Her mother and aunt blocked the door. "No, stay here. We don't want to appear to be too eager."

"Relax, Jenny." Jason came over and massaged her shoulders. "Dan and I have been over this a hundred times. He's got it under control."

The doorbell rang, and the house fell silent.

Her mother smoothed out the same pink *áo dài* Tam had brought back from Vietnam. At least it was getting some use, and it looked far better on Phuong than on her. "Your father and I must receive our guests. Do not come out until we come get you."

From the confines of her bedroom, Jenny strained to hear the conversation outside. Her parents opened the door and greeted Dan's family. Dan and his mother would be at the head of the procession. Maureen would ask permission of her parents for her hand, and Dan would present the first gift if they accepted, followed by each of his brothers and Paul. One of her cousins dressed in a red *áo dài* would receive each gift until they'd all been given. Only then would her parents send for her.

Heavy footsteps came down the hallway. Jenny checked her reflection, noting her flushed cheeks and full lips. She looked like a proper bride from the waist up.

Her stomach tightened again, bringing tears to her eyes this time. As soon as the ceremony was over, she needed to find a place where she could rest and rehydrate. But her parents stood in the doorway to retrieve her, so she told herself that could wait. Right now, all she wanted was to make her engagement to Dan official.

Dan's brothers towered over her family, making them easy to spot in the crowd. They were dressed in dark suits according to tradition and stood in line behind him.

The glow in Dan's eyes as she entered the room made her forget about her jitters. He looked at her like she was the most beautiful woman in the room, and her heart fluttered.

Just like he had at Chinese New Year, her father linked her hand with Dan's. "We present to you our daughter, Hue, to be your bride."

Dan squeezed her hand and followed her to the family altar, helping her down to her knees so they could pray for the ancestors' blessing. Another contraction hit her midway through the prayers, this one more intense than the earlier ones. She bit her bottom lip to keep from gasping, but Dan noticed it.

"The baby?" he whispered

She gave him a discreet nod.

"How far apart?"

"No idea."

"Then let's hurry this up and get you to the hospital." He stood and helped her up.

That was when another contraction ripped through her lower stomach. She clutched her belly, and dug her fingers into Dan's arms. The pain lasted less than a minute, but the gush of fluid that followed made her head swim.

Her water had just broken.

Her mother and Maureen rushed to her side, hiding the puddle that was trickling down her leg and forming around her foot. "Babies always know how to make their presence known, huh?" Maureen joked.

"I told you this would be a lucky day." Her mother wrapped her arm around Jenny's waist and helped her through the crowd. "My granddaughter will be arriving soon."

"I'll go get the car." Dan brushed by them, followed by his red-headed brother, Frank. He had the engine roaring by the time they got to the car.

Frank held the door open for them. "And here I was looking forward to getting to know your cute little cousins better," he said with a wink.

"Franklin Scott Kelly, you will behave yourself," his mother warned.

"But they're so cute and dainty."

Jenny wanted to warn Frank that her cousins just looked cute and dainty. They'd pack a mean wallop if he tried anything, followed by a not so pleasant reprimand from their fathers and brothers. But the next contraction took away her breath.

Jason and Mike's car pulled up alongside them. "We'll meet you at the hospital," Mike said in his calm courtroom voice.

She nodded and turned to Maureen. All the travel and preparations for the engagement ceremony were wasted now. "I'm so sorry for this. You came all this way, and we didn't even get to the dinner."

"We will have time to celebrate later," Phuong answered. "Right now, it is time for the baby. We will entertain our guests." Then, in an uncharacteristic show of affection, she kissed Jenny's cheek and turned to Dan. "Take care of my daughter and my granddaughter."

Dan met her mother's gaze and said solemnly, "I will."

***

Dan sped through the traffic on the freeway, his gaze shifting to his silent fiancée every thirty seconds. Jenny drew in a sharp breath through her nose, held it until her face turned red, and then exhaled with a slow sigh. He glanced the clock on the dash. The contractions were about three minutes apart now. If he didn't get her to the hospital soon, she was in danger of having the baby in the car.

And for a baby with gastroschisis, that could be dangerous. The risk of infection alone could kill it, not to mention the cold Seattle weather.

He rammed the accelerator until the speedometer teetered over seventy-five.

"Slow down, Dan. We don't want to have an accident."

"The HOV lane is clear."

"And what if a cop pulls us over?"

"Then I'll ask him if he wants to catch the baby."

The words came out light and jovially in stark contrast to the dark panic sludging inside his gut. He'd lead the cop on a merry chase straight to Labor & Delivery before he stopped. He wasn't going to risk anything with Jenny's baby.

As the skyline of Bellevue appeared, Jenny closed her eyes and cradled her stomach. "I'm not ready to let go of her yet."

Neither was he.

Even though his brain reminded him that this wasn't his child, he was still connected to her as though she did share his DNA. He wanted to hold her, watch her take her first steps, see her off to the prom and graduation. He wanted to be her father.

But like Jenny, he'd have to let her go to her real father as soon as she was born.

He blindly reached over and held Jenny's hand. "We'll still be here for her. It's not like she's leaving us to go to a perfect stranger."

Jenny nodded, her eyes still squeezed shut. "I know, but it's just not the same."

He ran his thumb over the top of her palm, knowing exactly how she felt at the moment.

***

Mike stood next to a nurse waiting with a wheelchair at the elevator that led from the parking garage straight to L&D. As soon as Dan skidded to a stop, he opened the door and helped Jenny out. "Jason's parking the car. We called ahead and let them know we were coming."

"Thank you." After the adrenaline-pumping race to the hospital, she was looking forward to the slow roll to the delivery suite. "Is my OB, Dr. Davis, here? What about the perinatologist?"

"We're getting everything in place for your baby's arrival," the nurse reassured her. "But first, we're going to get you changed into a comfortable gown and see how she's doing."

Jenny lowered her eyes to her ruined *áo dài*. She must look like some poor creature from a horror flick.

Another contraction rolled through her uterus. She gripped the arms of the wheelchair and clamped her jaw closed. Perspiration beaded along her scalp. She refused to scream or make a spectacle of herself in front of everyone.

Even though it was more painful than the time she broke her arm as a child, it would only last for a few seconds. She could get through it.

"How far apart are the contractions?" the nurse asked.

"Three minutes," Dan answered from behind them. "And from the look of things, getting more intense."

How did he read her as well as he did? She'd been trying so hard to keep up a brave face, to be stoic and deal with the pain through deep breathing.

But the last contraction seemed to linger in the form of an intense pressure building in her bottom. It wasn't exactly painful, but it wasn't comfortable either.

By the time they reached the delivery suite, Jason had joined them. The nurse looked at the crowd of men, confusion hazing her eyes. "Which one of you is the father?"

Mike stepped forward. "I am, but Dan is her fiancée."

The confusion only deepened the lines between the nurse's brows. "Um, well, I'm going to help her get undressed…"

"Message received loud and clear." Jason looped his arm through Mike's and led him toward the door. "We'll be out in the hallway until it's safe to come back in."

Jenny's legs trembled as she tried to stand. Dan steadied her as another contraction ripped through her. White-hot fire burned along the bottom of her pelvis, and the pressure intensified. As soon as she could speak, she said, "Please, can I go to the bathroom first? I feel like I need to go."

"No!" Dan and the nurse said in unison as they forced her into the bed.

"But the pressure…"

"Don't push." The nurse went to the phone on the wall and asked for assistance.

Jenny's heart swelled with panic. She turned to Dan. "What's going on?"

"When a woman in labor feels the need to push like that, it usually means you're fully dilated." He brushed her sweat-damp hair out of her face. "I can't tell you how many stories I heard during my OB rotation about babies being delivered in the bathroom."

The last thing she wanted was for her daughter to be born in a toilet.

No, it's not my daughter. It's Mike and Jason's. "I'll try not to push, then."

Three more nurses rushed into the room. One of them opened a closet to reveal a baby warmer, while the other two cut away the pants of her *áo dài*. The nurse who brought her to the room strapped a monitor to her belly and started typing information in the computer. It was a well-orchestrated dance, one the nurses had performed more than once, and some of Jenny's fear ebbed. Even if her daughter was born this second, the team would know what to do.

The nurses at her sides draped a sheet across her lap and then helped her bend her knees. One of them moved to the foot of the bed. "She's crowning."

Before she could ask if that meant what she thought it meant, another contraction slammed into her. A ring of fire burned between her legs. The primal urge to push threatened to overwhelm her. Every muscle in her body quivered from fighting it.

187

The door slammed open, and Dr. Davis ran in, half gowned. "The little girl decided to make an early appearance, eh?"

"During her engagement ceremony, no less," Jason said from the doorway.

The nurse who roomed them handed Mike a gown and a set of gloves. "Since you're the father, put these on. It's the only way they'll let you go near the baby."

Jenny searched the room and noticed that the nurses gathered around the warmer were wearing similar gowns and gloves. Everyone was taking special precautions for her daughter.

She inwardly winced every time she referred to the child inside her as her daughter. It wasn't hers. And yet, after all these months, how could she *not* be hers?

Dr. Davis finished tying on her gown and sat down on the stool at the foot of the bed. "Okay, Jenny, at the start of the next contraction, I want you to push."

Finally, they were going to let her do something about the pressure.

Dan took her hand and kissed her cheek. "You can do this."

She gave him a hesitant smile. He may have thought she could, but her strength was already zapped. The idea of pushing out a whole baby from such a small opening terrified her.

Another person in a blue gown and mask stepped into the room. "Am I too late?" he asked.

Jeez, it was turning into a three-ring circus. How many more people could they fit into this tiny room?

"Dr. Glanville, you're just in time," Dr. Davis replied.

"We're crowning, and I have a feeling this little girl will be out in one to two pushes."

The other doctor checked out the warming stand. "We're ready for her over here."

I'm not ready for this. I'm not ready to let her go.

The next contraction interrupted her thoughts and blurred her vision in a sea of black and white stars. She heard the distant command to push. Dan and one of the nurses supported her back while she bore down. Fire flared through her veins. So hot. So intense. So breathtaking and dizzying at the same time. She poured every ounce of her strength into that push.

And then a clammy rush of relief followed.

As her vision came back into focus, Dr. Davis was delivering something to the blue-gowned people gathered around the warmer. Mike stood behind them, his camera angled down to record what they were doing. A weak cry rose from the noise.

"Congratulations, Jenny," Dan whispered by her ear. "She's here."

"She's so beautiful, Jenny," Mike added, his eyes never leaving his daughter.

The crew of blue-gowned people started to move. Dr. Glanville pulled away to say, "We're going to take her down to the NICU and get her ready to go to Children's. Her father can come with us."

The warmer rolled out of the room, completely barricaded by the army of nurses. Mike followed, and the room started to clear out.

They never let me see her.

The realization punched her right in the center of her

chest. She'd given birth to her daughter, and she hadn't been allowed to see her, to hold her, to reassure herself this wasn't all just some bad dream.

She turned to find Dan staring at the door with grief tugging at the corners of his mouth and a wistful light in his eyes. He still held her in his arms, still held her hand in his, but his attention was focused on the child who'd been whisked out of the room before they'd even had a chance to know her.

Worry nagged at her insides. "Was the gastroschisis worse than we thought?"

"Not at all, Jenny," Dr. Davis replied from her position at the foot of the bed. "In fact, it was one of the smaller ones I've seen."

"So she'll be all right?"

"I'll defer to Dr. Glanville on that one, especially since she's a few weeks early, but I can tell you I've delivered babies with larger defects, and they turned out just fine." The doctor stood and removed her bloody gloves. "You got through this like a champ. No tears or anything."

The praise did little to comfort her. She still wanted her daughter back.

Dr. Davis left, leaving only the nurse who'd roomed them behind. She typed away at her computer, not saying anything to them as she charted.

Jenny turned back to Dan and stroked his cheek. "Did you get a glimpse of her?"

"Barely." He gave her a weak smile. "She has a head full of dark hair."

"Pretty normal for Vietnamese babies."

He nodded and stroked her hair. When he met her

190

gaze, an unspoken promise passed between them, one full of love and hope. It soothed the ache in her heart and gave her something to cling to in the coming years.

Next time, it will be ours.

Dan was here for her, both now and forever, and in that moment, she was finally able to let go of the regret that she'd carried throughout her pregnancy.

A soft knock came from the door, and Jason peered in. "Are you decent?"

Part of her wanted to laugh. She was still wearing the top part of her red *áo dài* from the engagement ceremony.

Dan pulled the covers up to her waist. "Come on in."

The door opened, and the gentle roll of a wheeled cart followed.

"We thought you'd like to see the baby before we leave," Jason said.

They brought the plastic incubator up to the bed, and Jenny's eyes welled up with tears. A tiny baby rested inside. A blanket covered her stomach, but it couldn't hide the abnormal bulge of bowel underneath. Tubes ran from the baby's nose and arms, and the soft frantic beep of a monitor announced every rapid beat of her young heart.

And yet, despite the reminders that this was a special-needs infant, she couldn't have been more beautiful. Jenny studied her face in awe, noting the almond shaped eyes and full lips. A pair of midnight black eyes blinked up at her as though the infant knew she was her mother. And the connection Jenny both feared and longed for formed.

"May I touch her?"

The nurse twisted open one of the side ports and nodded. "Just be gentle."

Jenny reached in and stroked her daughter's head. The hair was as fine as silk, dark and thick. She continued down until she got to the infant's hand. Immediately, her daughter clamped around her finger, and tears welled up in Jenny's eyes.

"I didn't think I'd ever fall in love with a woman," Mike said from the other side of the incubator, "but one look at her and I was gone."

Dan stood up to see better and then dropped another kiss on Jenny's cheek. "She's as beautiful as her mother."

Jenny's gaze never wavered from her daughter and the tiny hand gripping at her finger. "Have you picked out a name for her?"

"Camille," Mike replied, his voice choking up.

"Be good and come home to us soon, Camille," she said softly before she withdrew her hand.

The nurse twisted the port back into place and headed for the door.

"We'll send you pictures on the way over," Mike promised before following the team.

Jason gave her a hug. "Thank you again, sis. You've given the world to us, and you have no idea how grateful we are."

"I have an idea." She returned his hug and settled back against the pillows. "Keep me posted."

"We will." Jason left, and it was back to her, Dan, and the nurse in the room.

The nurse finally stepped away from her computer. "Let me get you a clean gown to change into."

When she disappeared into the bathroom, Jenny said, "Have I told you how much I love you today?"

"No, but we could try doing a Vulcan mind meld so we won't have to waste any time with words." He grinned, his eyes crinkling. "I love you, Jenny, and I look forward to spending the rest of my life with you."

"I love you, too, Dan." She tucked her head under his chin and rested her hand over his heart. "Thank you for being everything that you are."

"Only for you."

Chapter Seventeen

Dan tugged at the mustard yellow Starfleet shirt and searched the crowded convention lobby for Jenny. As much as he hated being dressed like Captain Kirk today, it was totally worth it after yesterday. A little over four months after having Camille, Jenny had been smokin' hot dressed in Princess Leia's gold bikini. He'd fought the urge to punch the endless stream of geeks who ogled his wife at the San Diego Comic-Con. The only thing that kept his jealousy in check was the knowledge that at the end of the night, he was the one who'd be making love to her.

Of course, there'd been a couple of quickies thrown in during the day to satisfy his own desires.

But since she'd agreed to dress as Leia to his Han Solo, he now had to dress as Kirk to her Uhura. At least the role play kept the first leg of their honeymoon interesting. As soon as Comic-Con was over, they were headed to Maui for the second leg of their honeymoon.

His phone buzzed in his pocket, followed by the sound of Uhura from the original series saying, "Come in, Captain."

He pulled it out to see a text message from Jenny.

"It seems we have an alien life form on board."

He clicked on the picture attachment, and the image of a positive pregnancy test filled the screen.

His head swam, and he stumbled back a step. As soon as her OB gave them the green light, they started trying to conceive, but he didn't expect her to get pregnant so quickly. The same mixture of joy and dread and apprehension rushed through him like the last time, followed by one difference.

This time, he actually looked forward to finding out he was going to become a father.

"Dan?"

The sound of Jenny's voice pulled him from his haze. She stood in front of him, her short red dress clinging to every tempting curve of her body. He pulled her into his arms and let everyone around them know she was his by his kiss.

"I take it you got my message?" she asked when he finally pulled away.

He nodded. "When was that picture taken?"

"Just now. That's why I was running a bit late this morning." She grinned up him, her dark eyes dancing with joy. "Are you ready for the next part of our voyage together?"

"Absolutely," he replied before he kissed her one more time.

A Note to Readers

Dear Reader,

Thank you so much for reading *The Heart's Game*. I hope you enjoyed it and look forward to the next book in the series, *A Seductive Melody*. If you did, please leave a review at the store where you bought this book or on Goodreads.

I love to hear from readers. You can find me on Facebook and Twitter, or you can email me using the contact form on my website, CristaMcHugh.com.

If you would like to be the first to know about new releases or be entered into exclusive contests, please sign up for my newsletter using the contact form on my website at bit.ly/19EJAW8.

Also, please like my Facebook page for more excerpts and teasers from upcoming books. And, just for this series, I have a special website featuring more information on the Kelly Brothers, playlists, recipes, and other extras just for readers. Please check it out at thekellybrothers.cristamchugh.com.

--Crista

Don't miss the next book in the Kelly Brothers series…

A Seductive Melody

Ethan Kelly lost his best friend and bandmate to an overdose, but staying clean is proving harder than he thought it would be. His only safety net during his first weeks of sobriety is his sponsor, Becca. As she guides him through the darkness, he begins to trust her not only with his secrets, but also his heart.

After years of trying to be the daughter her socialite parents wanted her to be (and failing miserably), Rebecca Shore finally has her life on track. Sure, she's interning at *Moderne* magazine when she'd rather be pursuing more serious journalism, but it's a foot in the door. She's just waiting for the scoop of a lifetime that will take her to the next level. But when she's asked to be the sponsor of the reclusive and enigmatic rock star, her heart is torn between the career she's always wanted and the fragile man who bares his soul to her.

Coming September 2014

Author Bio

Growing up in small town Alabama, Crista relied on storytelling as a natural way for her to pass the time and keep her two younger sisters entertained.

She currently lives in the Audi-filled suburbs of Seattle with her husband and two children, maintaining her alter ego of mild-mannered physician by day while she continues to pursue writing on nights and weekends.

Just for laughs, here are some of the jobs she's had in the past to pay the bills: barista, bartender, sommelier, stagehand, actress, morgue attendant, and autopsy assistant.

And she's also a recovering LARPer. (She blames it on her crazy college days)

For the latest updates, deleted scenes, and answers to any burning questions you have, please check out her webpage, CristaMcHugh.com.

Sign up for Crista's 99c New Release Newsletter at bit.ly/19EJAW8

Find Crista online at:

Twitter: twitter.com/crista_mchugh

Facebook: facebook.com/CristaMcHugh